CREE

The Rhys Davies
Short Story Award Anthology

T0158509

Rachel Trezise is a novelist and playwright from the Rhondda Valley. Her debut novel *In and Out of the Goldfish Bowl* won a place on the Orange Futures List in 2002. In 2006 her first short fiction collection *Fresh Apples* won the Dylan Thomas Prize. Her second short fiction collection *Cosmic Latte* won the Edge Hill Prize Readers Award in 2014. Her most recent play *Cotton Fingers* toured Ireland and Wales and won the Summerhall Lustrum Award at the Edinburgh Fringe in 2019. Her most recent novel *Easy Meat* came out in 2021. Twitter: @RachelTrezise

Originally from Belfast, Elaine Canning is a public engagement specialist, writer and editor living in Swansea, south Wales. She holds an MA and PhD in Hispanic Studies from Queen's University, Belfast and an MA in Creative Writing from Swansea University. She is currently Head of Special Projects at Swansea University and Executive Officer of the Dylan Thomas Prize. As well as having written a monograph and papers on Spanish Golden-Age drama, she has published several short stories. Her debut novel, *The Sandstone City*, publishes with Aderyn Press in November 2022. She is also editor of *Maggie O'Farrell: Contemporary Critical Perspectives* (forthcoming, Bloomsbury). Twitter: @elaine_canning

CREE

The Rhys Davies
Short Story Award Anthology

Edited by Elaine Canning
Selected and Introduced
by Rachel Trezise

PARTHIAN

Parthian, Cardigan SA43 1ED
www.parthianbooks.com
ISBN 978-1-914595-23-3
First published in 2022 © the contributors
Edited by Carly Holmes
Cover design by Syncopated Pandemonium
Typeset by Elaine Sharples www.typesetter.org.uk
Printed by 4edge Limited
Printed on FSC accredited paper

Contents

Introduction

Rachel Trezise

When I met my husband, from Clydach Vale, (at the other end of the Rhondda Valley to my own hometown, Treorchy) in January 2000, I noticed a blue plaque on the front of a house a little further along his street, an English Heritage commemoration to writer Rhys Davies who grew up in the greengrocer shop run by his father in the village, and after whom this competition is named. I have two very significant things in common with Rhys Davies. Firstly, we're both writers noted for our short stories despite also being novelists and playwrights, and secondly of course we both grew up in and chose to set much of our work in the Rhondda, a former coal mining area nestled in the centre of the south Wales valleys north of Cardiff, most famous for male voice choirs and rugby players.

I think the people of the Rhondda lend themselves particularly well to characters in literary and dramatic works, short stories in particular. As Irish short story writer Frank O'Connor explained in his study on the short story form, 'The Lonely Voice': 'Always in the short story there is this sense of outlawed figures wandering about the fringes of society hoping to escape from submerged population groups. As a result there is in the short story at its most characteristic something we do not often find in the novel – an intense awareness of human loneliness.' The Rhondda Valley at the time of Davies's youth was nothing if not a 'submerged population', the Depression of 1920 having finally reversed an industrial growth which had been in full flow for a hundred-and-fifty years. The south Wales coalfield, more dependent on exports than any other British mining area, was the worst hit.

Davies was apparently himself an 'outsider', quitter of school and chapel and a dandy who wore spats and carried a cane, who ate cake from his father's shop amid hunger-inducing mining strikes, a gay man living in the macho confines of coal country at a time when homosexuality was a criminal offence. Two of the stories in this anthology address the subject of being born homosexual in a loftily-heterosexual world. In 'Foolscap' Anthony Shapland fabricates a meeting between almost-strangers on a hill above the town; 'a play track for stunt bikes, a den, a place to get lost in, to disappear in, alongside siblings. Or away from them.' The rendezvous is hastily planned between characters simply called 'B' and 'M'. B knows how to be with other men; his brothers, his friends, his father, but now there's a new relationship to navigate, and a recognition of something he can't name. In 'Ghost Songs, 1985' Eryl Samuel employs pop culture to spell out the secret. Lloyd, bored on the picket line, snatches a listen to the Walkman he recently confiscated from his moping son: 'He pulls up his collar and strains to hear the lyrics, but all he can hear is someone repetitively screeching, *cry boy, cry boy, cry*. It's not Quo but at least it has an up-tempo beat...'

To my mind, Davies's finest skill was developing distinctive and believable characters, especially female characters, perhaps by closely observing women from his village in his father's grocery shop. Here, Matthew David Scott has written convincingly from the perspective of Jen, a record shop saleswoman striving to keep ends meeting in 'An Intervention'. Daniel Patrick Strogen has created the wonderfully complex and straight-talking Hefina, looking back on her younger life in '*Cracked*/Duck'. And in 'Splott Elvis and the Sundance Kid', Lindsay Gillespie has firmly established stammering runaway, Stu, both poignant and funny, and brilliant company. Much like in Davies's own work, the opposing themes of exile and belonging crop up in the anthology again and again, perhaps because south Wales, the valleys in particular, where most of these stories are set, has traditionally been the kind of place habitually left but very often returned to. Linette in Meredith Miller's 'Close in Time, Space or Order' comes back to Wales to look for her mother after decades camping on farms in Europe, only to find sleeping butterflies and newsletters from Greenham Common. 'He only said that because he needed her there,' Linette says of an old neighbour when he asks her not to leave again. 'They always need you in places like this. They want to watch you rise and fall.' In Matthew G. Rees's brilliant 'Endgame' a retired rugby ref, 'coastal belt now', returns to the valleys to officiate one last match. Suspecting someone from the club has poisoned his half-time tea, he paranoidly imagines their reasoning: 'Seen where this bastard's from? We'll teach him. Comin' up yer... bloody G-and-T-er!' But elsewhere he concedes: 'There was only *one* place on this earth where you were 'from'... the place that, when asked by others, you – or at least they – spoke of as your 'home' – the place where you were born... where you were schooled... the land – or that scarred, slagged patch of it – that was the land of your fathers and mothers. *That* was your home – no denying it, no shaking it off.'

There are also, however, other, more universal themes and topics. Grief, after the death of a family member as in Carys Shannon's 'Angel Face' and Bethan James's 'The Space

Between Pauses', or for part of your own self as in Satterday Shaw's heartbreaking 'My How To Guide' is impossible to avoid in literature and indeed life. But thankfully so is friendship, my favourite of all the themes in Laura Morris's winning story 'Cree'. It's here we watch a tired schoolteacher, Mrs Williams, develop an unusual camaraderie with one of her young pupils, Ben, who will remain her sole confidante when everything else in her life goes awry. The anthology is sometimes dark and emotional but always witty and acutely observed, the twelve shortlisted stories examining Welsh life, past and present, the strange games people play and the coping mechanisms they employ. A vivid portrait of the human condition in so very few words.

Cree

Laura Morris

Parents gather at the edge of the playground, not sure how close they should get to us – the teachers – as if we are strange beings from another time and place. Fathers send their children from the railings to the middle of the playground, ready to line up. Mothers get a little closer, teary, seeking reassurance from the eyes of others. A boy in Year 3, who reminds me of my Rhys, runs around the playground chasing the girls.

'I'm on cree-ee. You can't tag me,' one shouts.

Cree – the pre-determined safe place; the place where you can't get tagged – is, today, according to the children, the small patch of tarmac on the playground that's slightly lighter than the rest. When you are on cree, no one can get you. You are safe. You are home.

Year 6 stand on benches, carried out to the playground from the hall. The photographer's assistant shuffles and draws children, while the teachers take the seats at the front. John, the headmaster, surveys us, then joins the photograph. Deborah, the deputy, sits by his side.

'Knees together, ladies,' says the photographer.

Obediently, we snap our legs closed. The men are asked to sit with their legs apart, to make fists and place them on their knees. We smile, in unison say, 'Caerphilly cheese,' but in my head, I'm saying *just take the bloody picture.*

Later, I hand out exercise books, and tell the children to turn to the first page.

'Feel that paper with your hands,' I say. 'It's lovely and smooth, isn't it? I always think a fresh page is like a fresh start.'

The children look up at me. Waiting.

'Our theme for this year, Year 6, is The Future. We will be looking ahead to the Year 2000 and beyond – considering issues like science, technology, the environment, travel, and of course, any ideas you may have. Copy the date down neatly,' I say, tapping on *September, the fourth* with my whiteboard pen. 'Notice how we spell fourth. Remember the 'u'.'

There's too much noise coming from the classroom opposite: raised voices, laughter, the sound of chairs scraping across linoleum. I put my head around the door to find out what is going on. Sheets of newspaper, pots of glue and packets of straws are strewn over the tables.

'We are building bridges,' Emily, the new teacher, giggles. 'Literally and metaphorically.'

I smile, nod, and close the door.

'What are they doing?' asks Charlotte Evans, now out of her seat.

'Shhh.' I hold my finger to my lips.

The familiar feeling of pain behind my eyes.

John has set up a flipchart in front of the stage. He invites us to sit in a half circle, to peel a pink Post-it from the pack.

'What are we meant to be doing?' I ask Mari.

'We are writing down key words for the school's new mission statement.'

'Why can't we just say them out loud?'

'I think he's been on another course,' Mari whispers.

He invites us, one by one, to place our Post-its on the flipchart, to explain our chosen word to the room.

'Freedom,' I say. 'I don't think I need to explain that, do I?'

Emily's word is 'progress'.

John's word is 'standards'.

I have misunderstood the task.

'Deborah will gather all of the Post-its, collate the information, and get it typed up,' says John.

Deborah clicks her pen, writes in her new notebook.

'Number 2 on the agenda: the Christmas concert... I've been thinking,' John says, 'it's time for something new, something modern.'

'But... we always do the nativity... always,' I say, aware that I'm interrupting, aware that my voice is higher than it usually is.

'Last year, when training, I...' Emily begins.

'It's time for a change, Meryl. If you keep doing what you've always done, you'll keep getting what you've always got.'

'But the parents enjoy it,' I say.

'I'm sure the parents are just as bored as we are, Meryl.' He holds his pale hand to his mouth, performs an exaggerated yawn.

'But it's what Christmas is!'

'Deborah, if you could oversee the concert, please?'

Deborah nods, makes a *mm-hm* noise, and writes down John's instruction.

'Number 3 on the agenda: the inspection. We haven't had the exact dates yet, but we think it will be at the beginning of the spring term. Deborah has been in touch with a school in Gwynedd – inspected last March – and has learned that inspectors like to see original takes on theme work. Our themes are: Year 3 – Wales, Year 4 – Heroes and Villains, Year 5 – Animals, Year 6 – The Future. Creative ideas, please?'

'I thought we could dress up as dragons,' says Mel, 'for Wales.'

'Excellent,' says Deborah, repeating Mel's words slowly, before writing them down.

'What about Year 6?' I ask. 'The Future? They are a bit too old to dress up?'

'You could build a time machine,' suggests Emily.

'Yes,' everyone agrees. 'Great idea, Emily.'

I say nothing. I'm thinking of the mess, the time that constructing such a thing will take. But later, driving home, queueing at the Piccadilly lights, I realise that it is a good idea; it could elicit some wonderful writing from the children.

Rhys's halls are clean and modern, not like the digs I had in my first year at Aber. An en suite! I nod politely at other parents as we pass on the stairs with boxes. So much stuff piled up in the boot, but it doesn't look like a lot once we've unpacked and arranged his new life on the narrow shelves above the desk.

'If you get homesick, I will come to get you. I will pick you up,' I say. 'You know that.'

'He can get the *Trawscambria*,' says Bill.

'I will be fine, Mam.'

I want us to walk along the promenade, like Bill and I used to, but Rhys's new flatmates have asked him to drinks, and Bill isn't keen – 'The clouds are thick. Full of something,' he says, staring up at the darkening sky.

Bill drives his route home – short cuts, weak bridges, single lanes. The rain is heavy on the windscreen, becoming sleet. It's not at all like the October Dad drove me to Aber. Dry. Cool. Still. 1965. A blue and green checked coat, a knotted navy scarf flung freely over my shoulder.

Bill is singing. He's tapping out a rhythm on his knee.

I am shrieking. I am reaching for Bill's arm, telling him to brake.

There is a lamb lying in the middle of the road, a ewe nursing it.

'Do something!'

'Like what?'

The lamb is bleeding from its side, and the ewe is licking it. I try to guide the ewe to the side of the road, but it's bleating protectively, and won't leave its child. I pull up the hood of my raincoat to stop the rain getting in, but the wind keeps tugging it back down.

'Come on, Meryl. Leave it.'

I run around the side of the car, and take out the picnic blanket from the boot. I am trying to say, 'We can't leave it here,' but my throat can only make noises, noises that come from the deep of my belly.

I wrap the blanket around the lamb, and Bill helps me carry it to the side of the road. Neither of us speaks for the rest of the journey home, but he must know that I'm crying. *I sound like an animal*, I think. *I sound like the ewe.*

The children and I compile a list: broken watches and clocks, buttons, yogurt pots, tins, egg cartons, bubble wrap. We plan different designs for the time machine, and at the end of the session the new child, Ben, brings me a wonderfully ambitious diagram – neatly labelled. I'm not sure the end result will meet his vision, but I will endeavour.

I begin the work of assembling a frame out of cardboard

boxes and old wood. I use the glue gun to fix all of the sections together; then, putting down newspaper to catch the drips, I promise the children I will paint it during dinner time.

They unpack their sandwich boxes, collect coats from their hooks, but Ben stays behind.

'May I help you paint, Mrs Williams?' he asks.

'Of course,' I say, 'but wouldn't you rather play outside? It's a lovely autumnal day.'

'I would rather be doing this.'

I have noticed that when the other boys are playing rugby, Ben sits on the steps to the portacabin, reading.

'Well in that case, I had better find you a brush.'

Over dinner, Ben tells me about time dimensions. I listen patiently and never once say that these things he is explaining are not possible.

'And how do you know all of this?'

'I have some of the old *Doctor Who* annuals and my mother finds me the videos in charity shops.'

'Who is your favourite doctor?' I ask.

'John Pertwee, I think.'

I nod. I know who that one is.

'I'm going to eat my lunch now, Mrs Williams,' he says.

'Of course, Ben.'

He removes clingfilmed sandwiches from his tin; they are crustless, cut into perfect squares. He nibbles around the edges, until the square gets smaller and smaller, then eats his grapes, then the chopped apple, then his chocolate bar, splitting it into pieces first. He takes a sip of his drink.

'I don't like mixing foods in my mouth, Mrs Williams.'

'Neither do I, Ben, neither do I. Do you know what? You and I are *exactly* the same,' I say, sitting back at my desk, cleaning my glasses with the corner of my skirt.

'You may not know this about me, but I sometimes wear glasses,' Ben says.

'Oh.'

'But my father wears contact lenses, Mrs Williams. Have you ever tried them? I think you should – bring out your eyes a bit more. I sometimes feel they are hidden beneath your glasses.'

The optician's face is so close to mine that I can smell his skin. He asks me to rest my face in various contraptions, shines lights in front of my eyes. They unsettle me, these tests. Any sort of test. Afterwards, he leads me out of the room and sits me at a table on the shop floor. I watch him open a packet of lenses, and fish one out of its solution with his fingers.

He shows me how to hold my eye open with one hand, then how to pick up the lens with the other.

I get the lens quite close to my eyeball, but my eyelid is twitching.

'I'm sorry,' I say. 'It's difficult.'

'Try the other first,' he says. 'You might find it easier.' He glances at his watch.

'I have taken up too much of your time,' I say.

At home, I ask Bill if he notices anything different about me. He moves his tongue around his mouth, as if dislodging spinach from between teeth.

'New scarf?'

'I have contact lenses,' I say. 'I'm not wearing glasses.'

'Why?'

'Well…' I begin. 'It doesn't matter.'

That evening, I hear him on the phone in the spare room, where he now sleeps. His voice is low and soft, and I know he's talking to her.

Ben is standing outside the classroom, holding a Batman walkie-talkie. I am inside the time machine, holding its twin.

'Mrs Williams, can you hear me? Over.'

'I can hear you,' I say, adjusting Robin's aerial.

'I have been thinking… we need a control panel, otherwise how will the time machine work? Over.'

'Yes. Good idea.'

'Where would you go, Mrs Williams, if you could go anywhere? Over.'

'Now, I know that we are learning about the future, Ben, but I would go back in time, back to 1965,' I say. 'October 20th, 1965.'

'You need to say "over" when you have finished, Mrs Williams.'

'Sorry, Ben, of course. I'm not very good at this, am I? Over.'

'She keeps thinking she has told me things when she hasn't,' Dad tells me. 'Like the dentist this morning. Luckily, Mr Thomas understood, and fitted her in when we got there late.'

'I thought you were marking things on the calendar.'

'I try,' he says, 'but I forget too.'

Mam's in the living room, sitting in her armchair. There's a hot water bottle behind her, and weak tea trembling in the bone china cup.

'Rhys not with you?' she asks.

'He's at university, Mam.'

'Ah, yes, Swansea.'

'No, Mam. Aberystwyth. Remember?'

'Ah. Bet you regret not having another now? I told you that you'd be lonely.'

Back then, I kept a diary, and on October 21st, 1965, I wrote one word, and underlined it: <u>Bill</u>. Nothing else, just his name. I never wrote in the diary again, and I never kept a diary again, not one like that, not one for feelings.

I know now that there could have been other men. I know now that I married the wrong man.

Ben is sitting inside the time machine on a piano stool I brought in from the garage.

'Where will you go, Ben?'

'To the future,' he says.

'What is it like there?' I listen from outside.

'I'm not there yet. I haven't pressed the correct buttons.'

'Sorry, Ben,' I say. 'Silly me.'

That evening, at home, he writes a story about warring robots, and when he shows me the following morning, I look past the violence of his drawings, and focus on the ambitious vocabulary he has used. I take his work to my next progress meeting with Deborah.

'So,' she begins, 'who are your level 5s?'

'Well, Ben definitely. I mean, he's probably higher than a 5. I have been giving him books to read at home. He's read *Animal Farm*, and he understands the political allegory.'

'He can't be higher than a 5?'

'He is.'

'It stops at a 5. He can't be a 6 until secondary school.'

'I think he is. If you look at the criteria, especially for writing, he is doing it all. Listen: *You crouch behind a discarded shield, watching the battle from safety. The robot soldiers are quicker and stronger than any man, but despite their complex programming, they don't have the compassion of a human.* You see how he's used the second person here, and the present tense. I've not taught him those things. He's just doing them.'

'Yes. That is quite good. You should do that task with the class during inspection week. That would really impress them.'

'But he's already written it?'

'Yes, well he's *practised* it. He could do it again. Remember we discussed this in the meeting last week, *practising* tasks.'

'I'm not going to ask him to do it again.'

Deborah smiles at me.

'How are you, Meryl?'

'I'm okay, thank you.'

'How are *things*? *You know...*'

'Things?'

'Yes, you know... *things*.' Her charm bracelet jangles as she points her finger downwards. I think she is referring to my vagina, perhaps both of our vaginas, as if to say *you're a woman, and I'm a woman; we are in this together, you and me.*

'Are you referring to the menopause?' I ask.

'No, God no, but... I just wondered... Bill is doing well now, isn't he? Lots of concerts. I saw he has a new car.'

'Yes?' One of the charms is a gold cat with two staring emerald eyes.

'And I suppose you will be retiring soon. You know... I just wonder, do you need to work? Really?'

'I am only fifty-five, Deborah.'

She looks at her nails, and I stare at the abstract painting hanging on her office wall. Thick pink brush strokes.

'Meryl,' she begins.

'Yes.'

'Do you think I could ever be headteacher?'

It is the Christmas concert. There are children wearing black leotards, leggings, and tunics made of *Bacofoil* lurking around the school stage. They have been instructed to move slowly, to stretch out their arms, and to point, quite unsettlingly, into the audience. Swimming goggles sit uneasily on their heads, threatening to fall off with any sudden movement. At the end of the performance, I clap, and afterwards, when I'm pouring boiling water onto tea bags, and offering parents *Co-op* mince pies from a paper plate, I say how good their children were, how proud of them they should be. 'Aliens! In the nativity?' I say. 'Whatever next?'

Later, while Bill is playing at a Christmas concert at St David's Hall, I sit at the kitchen table, making additional features for the time machine – Ben's suggestions. I draw a large circle on a sheet of grey cardboard. With a thick black pen, in capital letters I write *PAST, PRESENT, FUTURE* on the circle. I cut the shape of an arrow from black paper and place it in the centre of the circle. I then push a brass fastener through, allowing me to spin the arrow.

Rhys sits opposite me, home from university for the holidays. He fiddles with my papers, picks up a marker pen, puts it down again.

'I need your help, Mam.'

'What is it?'

'I need to borrow money.'

'What for?'

'Not for me. Not really. It's for a procedure. It was a one-night thing.'

The pen is in his hand again. He's tapping it against the table.

'Oh, Rhys.'

'She wants it done as soon as possible. She doesn't want to wait until after Christmas.'

'No. I suppose she wouldn't.'

'Please don't tell Dad.'

'This is definitely what she wants too?'

'Yes.'

'Then I will go to the bank on Monday.'

He kisses my cheek and says goodnight quietly. I stay at the table, spinning the arrow from past to present to future.

From past.

To present.

To future.

Boxing Day, I continue preparing lessons. I also have books to mark, comprehension tasks to assess. I move the tins of chocolate and shortbread out of the way, and spread my work across the kitchen table.

'But it's Christmas, Mer,' says Bill.

'I know, but I won't fit everything in otherwise. There just isn't the time.'

The telephone rings, and we both turn our heads, as if that will be enough to silence it; like a crying baby, it continues.

'I'll take it upstairs,' Bill says, but it's too late. I've got there first.

'Hello.'

The other woman returns the receiver to its cradle.

'*But it's Christmas*, Bill,' I say.

A new year. The tiny ghosts that leave my mouth remind me I am still breathing. I turn on the electric heater, remove my gloves and run my hand over the smooth and cool wood of the desk. Age spots on my hands now. I don't remember the first wrinkle, the deepening of the lines on my forehead, the darkening of the shadows beneath my eyes, but there must have been a day when those things first appeared.

Inside the time machine, I use double-sided tape to fix Rhys's old calculator to the control panel. Next to that I stick the Dairy Diary calendar the milkman left with our clotted cream and orange juice on Christmas Eve. I attach a piece of string to a small hook and tie the string around a pen.

'We can circle the date we wish to travel to on the calendar,' I explain to Ben.

'A good idea,' he says. 'The time machine just needs one more thing.'

'Yes?'

Ben unzips his rucksack, takes out a controller.

'It's from my Nintendo 64,' he says, 'I don't need it anymore, Mrs Williams. I don't play those sorts of games now.'

'Oh Ben,' I say, 'only if you're sure.'

'I hope the inspectors like it, Mrs Williams.' Carefully, so that I understand the power of the object, he hands me the controller.

'Let's fire up the glue gun!'

Afterwards we step back, regarding the time machine proudly.

'It's even better than I thought it would be,' Ben says. 'It's almost… real.'

~~Phone the doctor~~
~~Pack a bag for Mam~~
~~Food shop for Dad~~
Flowers

'We are running a race,' John says to the children during assembly. 'We can see the finish line ahead of us, but we aren't there yet. It is important that we keep going and don't dip until the very end… which will be…' He pauses to flick through his notebook, looking for the inspection dates, 'in approximately a fortnight's time.'

'When's this race Mr Jones keeps talking about? I think I might win,' asks one of Emily's.

'What's a fortnight?' asks Ryan Thomas.

And all the time I am doing what they ask. We are practising the lessons and we are working on our spelling, writing better sentences, using connectives such as *additionally* and *on the other hand*. I sit with the weaker pupils, helping them write more accurately, dictating sentences to them, trying my hardest to get their work up to a level 4. I call them out one by one, listen to them read; I interview them, ask them their target levels, check that they know how to reach the next level. If they have been absent, then they stay in at break to catch up on the work they have missed. I trim their worksheets with the guillotine, I stick them to empty pages in their books. No gaps. There can't be any gaps. I mark their work, commenting on the positives, writing out targets for improvement. *Remember to use an apostrophe to show possession. Write in more detail, using a range of adjectives. 6x9 is 54, 7x9 is 63. Write two more sentences about Alun Michael.*

The caretaker wheels a computer on a trolley into my classroom, and Ben sets it up. He shows me how to use the Internet, and tells me that I can ask Jeeves anything, and he will give me an answer. When the children have all gone home, into the white box next to the cartoon man wearing a pinstriped suit, I type: *why do I feel so sad?*

I arrange Mam's flowers in a plain white vase, and she tells how, in the middle of the night, a woman at the other end of the ward calls out for her dead husband, Don. When I complain on her behalf, explain how Mam isn't sleeping, the nurse tells me that I should have more compassion.

'Imagine losing someone you love.'

I imagine Bill lying in the middle of a country road, bleeding from his side.

I drive Dad home, then drive myself home. I turn onto our drive, brake, turn off the engine, pull up the handbrake. There's a sound of something snapping, something small but significant, and the car begins to slide backwards down the drive, and into Bill's car.

'You have obviously been lifting the handbrake a little higher and higher each time,' says Bill when I go inside to tell him, 'and now, look what you've done.'

Before I bathe, trying to do a good, clean thing, I take fresh bedding into the spare room for him, but it has already been changed. I know she has been there, stood on my carpet, tidied her hair in my mirror, lay in my bed. This one has been in my home.

Four school inspectors line up awkwardly between the sink and fire extinguisher in the staffroom. They tell us that there is nothing to worry about, that they are only interested in facts, only interested in evidence, only interested in the truth. *They are not the same things*, I think. Afterwards we gather around the timetable that Deborah has pinned to the notice board. I will be observed three times over the week, starting with English.

The lesson begins with the lights dimmed, and *Tubular Bells* playing on the portable CD player. The children listen carefully to the music. 'How does it make you feel?' When I turn the lights on again, I notice one of the inspectors standing at the back of the classroom, holding a clipboard.

The children enter the time machine two by two. Then, inspired by the experience, they can write freely in whatever form they choose.

Ben is at the computer. He has chosen to write a newspaper article on cloning. He is laying it out in columns, and inserting pictures with witty captions. The inspector hovers over him as he writes.

At the end of the lesson, I ask him to read what he has written out to the class.

'Should I stand?' he asks.

'Yes,' I say. 'Why not?'

'Dolly the sheep was the first mammal to have been successfully cloned from an adult cell. Previous clonings have been from embryo cells. People now wonder whether this controversial technique could be used to clone humans, but many countries are banning it. I think that is a good thing. Imagine if someone cloned teaching inspectors, and all of us had one of them peering over our shoulder, as I've had today.'

I daren't look at the inspector's face, but I thank Ben for his clever piece of writing.

The children tidy up, ready for dinner time, but some ask to stay and finish what they are writing. Charlotte and Menna want to go back inside the time machine, but the inspector has asked to talk to me, so I ask the class to play outside. Even Ben.

'Thank you for the lesson, Mrs Williams,' he says. 'Now, the child, the boy at the computer? Is there something wrong with him?'

'Wrong with him?'

'Yes.'

'No, there's nothing wrong with him. He's highly intelligent.'

'I see. His article was a bit strange, wasn't it?'

'I thought it was very good.'

'Tell us about your lesson, Mrs Williams... the children

were writing for about half an hour, and I noticed that there wasn't really a plenary. Was there a reason for this?'

'Well, the children were really enjoying the writing.'

'Would you normally do that? Or would you normally close a lesson?'

'It depends really, on what we are doing. Sometimes we carry on after break or lunch. Sometimes we carry on with the work the next day.'

In some sort of shorthand that I can't decipher, he is writing down what I say.

'How do you set your end of Key Stage 2 targets?'

'I say what I think, and then Deborah tells me I'm wrong. She then sets new targets.'

'And what do you think about the new targets?'

'I think that they are too high for most children, but for a child such as Ben, they are often too low.'

'You have been here a long time, Mrs Williams. Do you enjoy your work?'

Do I enjoy my work?

'I attended this school myself,' I say. 'It was the Girls' Grammar School then, but the same building. I failed the 11+, well, that's what I was told, so I didn't start here straight away. I got in a year later – me and a girl called Jeanie Davies. You know, it was only recently I found out that in order for LEAs to offer an equal amount of places for girls and boys, the pass mark for boys was lower. Too many girls would have got in otherwise. Too many girls. My son, Rhys, he's studying sociology at university, and he told me. Had we been boys – Jeanie and I – we would have got in. Recently I've been wondering if Jeanie ever found that out, because I would like her to know that, like me, she didn't really fail the first time, that she *was* good enough, because feelings like that, feelings of failure – they stay with you, you know? Do I enjoy my work, you ask? Well, here's the thing: I have been teaching for nearly thirty years now, and while there are elements of it that remain rewarding, increasingly I feel as with the cruelest types of diseases, teaching is killing me slowly.'

The inspector stops writing. He removes his glasses, rubs his eyes, looks at me, and thanks me for my time.

Sharp pain across one eye, and in the back of my head now.

I return to my desk, sit down. There's a crackle from the Robin walkie-talkie.

'Mrs Williams, are you there? Over.'

I pick up.

'Ben?'

'The kids!' says Ben. 'They were too rough with the time machine. Some things have fallen off, but I will glue them back on for you when I'm allowed back in. Over.'

'Thank you, Ben.'

Fingers on eyelids, applying pressure.

'Did the inspector like our lesson? Over,' Ben asks.

'I don't think he did, Ben.'

Fingers on temples, then clawing skull.

'I am sorry about that, Mrs Williams. I know how hard you have worked.'

'Thank you, Ben.'

'Mrs Williams, Mr Jones is crossing the playground. Mrs Pugh is with him too. Over.'

'They are coming over here? To my room?'

'I think so. Over.'

'Oh Ben, why won't everyone just leave me alone?'

'Mrs Williams, you need to get into the time machine,' Ben says. 'Trust me.'

I step inside the time machine, and sit on the piano stool,

my back against the heavy cardboard. There is no more time now. Sand through an hourglass. Finger on my lips. 'Shh.' Listen to the children playing outside; listen to Bill's soft telephone voice – a voice he no longer uses for me; listen to the woman opposite Mam at the hospital, calling out for her dead husband; listen to the mournful bleating of the ewe, miles and miles away in Ceredigion.

Static hissing, radio waves travelling at the speed of light, electric currents, loudspeaker, then Ben's voice – clear and kind. Ben will tell me what to do, and I will do as Ben says.

Endgame

Matthew G. Rees

THE mist is dense now. No longer a matter of mere wisps and patches, its strands and its gauzes have woven together... and advance through the darkness as one.

A twist in the road, and his headlights – their strange, smoky beams – fall for a moment on some firs. The trees are like conspirators... of the kind who've been caught in an alley, with the loft of a watchman's lamp.

His lights swing away from them, back to the mist's white wall.

He tries full beam against it.

As if magnetised, the mist bounds to the edge of his bonnet – smothering... sparkling... a stifling, swirling blanket of liquid crystals of light.

He quickly switches back to dipped.

At the sides of the road, bracken shows once more.

Ahead of him: yardage... a breathing space, restored.

Shit! If only he'd known.

And yet... he *had* known – of course.

This was how it was – how it always had been – on the mountain road at night. The mist – the *niwl*... for those who spoke of it in the other tongue. Its treacherous cloak: the reason people drove *up* the valley rather than going 'over the top'. Oh, it would be down there, too, on a night like this. But in the

24

valley there'd be streetlamps, the lights of Spars, fish bars, pubs. He remembers them: The Colliers... The Railway... The Lamb. Some still in business... surely?

Behind him, on the dual carriageway, there'd been no mist at all.

It had only shown itself after the sheep grid that came after the turn-off: the rattle under his wheels almost 'whistling it up'... 'tapping its shoulder', so it seemed.

It's as if – till now – it must have been looking... *feeling*... for someone else. But now it had *him*... had settled on *him*.

Suddenly, on the car's offside, the thump of something hard under his front wheel. And the same, almost immediately, under the back.

It startles him, but he thinks: *Cat's eye... I'm drifting. Still, the road's there, at least.*

Anyway, it was this way now – over the top – if he was to make it... to get there at all.

***

He'd had his doubts about accepting it – the game – from the start.

The phone call had caught him off-guard: the voice at the other end not one that he knew.

The caller had given a name, or seemed to, only for a kink in the connection to blank it out as he spoke.

The guy said he was sorry for the late notice, but they could find no one else. All they needed to know – at District – was whether he could do it, help them out. As far as they were concerned, that would be the end of things: he'd be finished for good after that.

In replying, he'd been hesitant. It was difficult, he said... he had commitments. Besides, he was supposed to have retired. He'd written and told them all of that at District. They'd had his email weeks ago. So —

Shitting hell!!

Suddenly, now, in his headlights: a sheep... middle of the road... right in front of him.

He stomps the footbrake and clutch, flies forward... is stopped and snatched back by the belt.

Within a split second, the weight of the car catches up with him, slamming into his shoulders and spine.

Meanwhile, the sheep stands there, and stares.

In the beam of his headlights, distinct in the darkness, the animal seems oddly large.

It eyes him.

It is thin, ragged, grey, but also... calm, aloof.

A tatty rosette of red aerosol lies, like an open wound, on a haunch that has little if anything in terms of a fleece.

It is wholly unlike the sheep he sometimes sees while driving near his home... in the fields and on the saltmarsh of the estuary.

In its eyes, there is something... *resentful*, he thinks.

He fancies he sees the amber irises... the black slits.

Its ugly jaw grinds.

It wanders on. Disappears.

With a curse, he releases the clutch, continues to drive... disentangles his thoughts.

So... he'd told the guy – was it Dai? Doug? He'd told him... 'Yes... okay. But this has to be the last.' After which, the other man's manner had been brisk, down-to-business, stripped of all pleading: 'You'll be doing...'

The names of the villages fell from him quickly – like roof slates, deliberately dislodged.

No wonder no one had wanted to know. No wonder they'd come begging to him.

'Cup match, technically,' the doer of the District's dirty work had breezed. 'But the other results in the group mean it's a dead rubber. Pointless, really. Still, it's got to be done.'

He'd wanted to answer: 'Thanks. That's some way to bow out.'

But he said nothing, sensing that the messenger – 'hospital pass' safely made – had already cut and run.

***

His car has ceased climbing. Glimpses of stone ruins that were once livestock pens and lime kilns tell him he's on 'the top': the moor… the *rhos*.

He crawls at twenty, into the mist, which, if anything, is heavier here, the relative flatness allowing it to settle and spread.

Like gas, he thinks.

Branches of ancient, hunched trees claw at the night.

The palms of his hands are moist on the wheel.

***

In time, the temperature gauge rises – one degree, and then another – in the pale blue digits on the dash.

His course has become a weaving one. And he knows that he's dropping down: on the mountain's other side – the inner side… the valley side.

He takes the hairpins gently, sensing (from distant memory) where they wait.

In places, the mist not only thins but parts.

Through a hole, he sees the village: orange specks of

streetlights pricking tubular silhouettes of terraced houses – their stony faces strung entrenched on the opposite hillside.

And – never mind that he's 'coastal belt' now... has been for years: bay views from his windows – he recognises it... *knows* the old place, of course.

After a moment, a drift of the mist seals the gap, veils the view, returns the scene to his past.

***

The nose of his car is undeniably downward now. Conscious (although he cannot see it) of the drop to his side, he continues – gingerly – his zig-zag descent.

Without warning, in the tight curve of a hairpin, he catches sight of it: The Ground.

It sits there... lit-up, proud.

It's as if someone has thrown a switch – just for him.

In the bright light, the 'arena' looks orderly... clean.

Yet, even at that distance, he seems to see the rotting woodwork; the moss; the rust. He feels – or thinks he does – the dripping leaks in the corrugated sheds that some called 'stands'; the bitter, freeze-your-balls-off cold of the stark, steepling terraces.

For a second or so, in his car, he shivers.

A movement of the mist conceals everything, as if an eye has shut.

***

The shudder of a sheep grid confirms that he's 'down'.

The mist releases him into a scrub of half-fallen fenceposts, old oil drums, nettles and ferns.

Beyond it: the first roofs and walls.

A streetlamp spills light onto the seat beside him… the steel whistle that waits there.

Dead rubber?

Be damned!

***

In the car park at the ground: potholes filled with water… axles lumbering over them. Dark figures, plumes of breath, tangerine tips of cigarettes. Laughter… of a kind.

'Edge' of an evening match, fought mid-week.

He knows the signs.

Forget your Saturday 'sport', this is the coalface… this is where the dirty stuff gets done: a dead-end village at the top of a valley that has no police, no panda cars, for miles. In so far as any law exists here, I – tonight am it.

***

No one greets him. They don't have to. He knows the way.

Change? You never found it in a place like this. Just blokes who drank in the same clubs as their grandfathers, voted like them, proud of it, too.

By some bloody miracle, he'd got out. 'Coastal belt… gin-and-tonic set.' Well, fair enough, maybe that's what he'd become. But what the hell was left up here? Ghosts? Scrap? If that?

And yet…

There was only *one* place on this earth where you were 'from'… the place that, when asked by others, you – or at least they – spoke of as your 'home' – the place where you were born... where you were schooled... the land – or that scarred, slagged patch of it – that was the land of your fathers and mothers. *That* was your home – no denying it, no shaking it off.

***

He undresses now, does some warm-ups – stretches, bends – in his pants.

Shithole of a changing room, of course.

Black mould on the shower curtain, no paper in the WC. Stud-holed mud with wire-grass tufts – not swept since last summer, by the looks – littering the floor.

He observes himself in the mirror – cracked on the breeze block wall.

How long since he was last here? Ten years? More? He looks older. Who wouldn't? But in reasonable shape for a man of his age. Sunday runs on the seafront. Golf – eighteen holes and no buggy – once a week.

From beyond his chamber, the stamp of studs; shouts, semi-muffled; the calling of names: 'Stevie... Griff.' And, increasingly, urgings to war: 'Come on now, boys! Let's *bloody* do it!!'

His socks go on first. He's always started with them.

Last, his shirt.

He thinks, for a moment, how it would have been nice to have worn the one from his very first game. He still has it. At home. Even now, it would probably fit. 'Home' – the other home, the one that he'd made. How remote it seemed: his wife, his kids (all grown-up, leaving soon, no doubt).

He checks his watch. Five minutes and he'll call the captains out for 'a word'. Not that it will make much difference, but he'll say it anyway. How he's sent their fathers off and – in some cases – their grandfathers, and, if need be, he won't hesitate to do the same with them. Never mind it being his last match: the laws of the game will be upheld. That's one thing they *can* be sure of.

Boots now. He pulls his laces tight, ties them.

He winds his spare watch and straps it to his wrist. Cards, pencil and notebook in the right pocket of his shorts. Lawbook in the left. An ancient, dog-eared one, admitted. An old lawbook for an old lawman. *It rings right,* he thinks.

There's 'history' up here, after all. Money at the root, in the main. His hosts had once been kicked out of the Union, renegades who joined the Northern cause. For the visitors, a more recent matter: 'bungs', as the soccer boys called them… to players with a bit of flair, or who were known as 'hardmen', to lure them – from other clubs – onto the team-sheet in time for some fixture of the 'crunch' kind, on which fortunes might turn.

And then there was the history between the clubs: the head-stamping, eye-gouging, scrotum-ripping, leg-breaking, ear-biting, lung-puncturing 'history' – if that was the word; something that wasn't a mere battle for valley bragging rights, but a full-on, full-bore, blood feud.

No one at District or the Union had ever wanted to know. 'Let the buggers get on with it… Who the hell wants to go poking their noses in up there?'

If you drew the short straw and got given a game with either, you just did your eighty, got off and got out – sharpish. Only a fool bothered with injury-time… frills like 'time off' and 'time on'. You just blew your bloody whistle – and went.

He ties his whistle to his wrist.

The cord is an old red lace (and he thinks – for a moment –

about the way in which it is… umbilical). He feels the metal – cold and hard – in his grip.

And he steps out, into the tunnel.

***

The tunnel lies empty, like an underpass on a 'bad' estate. He's not heard the players go. But he knows – from the reek – that they've been there.

At its end, the mouth and the pitch beckon.

Butterflies now – same as ever – in his belly.

No turning back though… someone must do this… be the man in the middle. How else will the game go on?

Clatter of his studs on the concrete floor – their *ank ank ank* made loud by the absence of others.

Close to the end, and just before the field, comes a disembodied voice (and a civility that surprises him). 'Good evening, sir.' At the same time, shadowed hands place in his a ball.

Four more strides and he's out there: damp film of the night air on his face.

His senses are struck by the scintillations of the dew-soaked grass. The floodlights fill each wet stalk with radiance.

***

The players are there. Waiting.

Little – if any – acknowledgement from them.

He summons the captains, and they walk to where he positions himself: on the halfway line, centre-field.

He considers them as they advance.

Two 24-carat bruisers, if ever there were – a second-row

who's a chimneystack of scar tissue, and a hooker, all beer-gut (swinging low), with a face seemingly stuck in a gargoyle gurn, ears so purple, torn and barely 'there' that it looks as if sewing their scraps back on – ham-fisted, with needle-and-thread – is his restful Sunday hobby after ale-soaked Saturday nights.

The planned pep talk is something he decides to forget, judging it best to just get things done.

He tosses his tenpence.

The home captain clears his nostrils of snot.

The visiting skipper takes out his gumshield (to reveal an absence of teeth) and calls.

'Stay as we are,' he slurs, after it lands – *heads* – on the grass.

They return to their ends.

He thinks: *Only one thing on their agendas: getting stuck in.*

The home side's fly-half comes up to kick off: a youngster who heels at the turf old-style and places the ball.

He notices that the lad's right hand has only two fingers – stumps near the knuckles where the others have been shorn.

The boy steps back and waits for his whistle…

Set to blow, he glances left and right, ears ready for the battle cries – the Remember-the-Alamoes; the kick-it-to-those-bastards, boys – that he expects – any second – to be bawled from the teeming sheds and the spilling terraces… the screams and yells swelling to a tsunami of noise, a savage blood-baying roar.

And yet he hears… almost nothing.

There are – at best – mere splinters of sound; urgings that – to him – seem half-hearted… hollow. Their isolation sends them echoing around the ground.

And it's now that he notices that the arena, this unlovely fortress of the upper valley, this 'Colosseum of Cruelty' as once christened, which, before now, has fed the appetites of five thousand, is – to all intents and purposes – empty.

His whistle shrills the air.

***

From the No 10's kick, the ball – via a fumble – spills into touch.

First line-out, seven seconds in.

Right – this is when things really *start. Here we bloody go. They'll* all *be at it: elbows into noses, knees to ribs, boots to bollocks. 'Retaliation in first.' Too many to penalise any single offender, of course: why they called them 'packs': how they went hunting. Their free-for-all will leave him no option. Riot Act: general warning. Next bloke who takes a swing: off.*

And yet, when the ball is lobbed-in from the touchline, the scar-faced lock palms it – smoothly, without incident – and, from the halves, the white oval moves out – cleanly and sweetly – along the line.

A thin blade of a boy, on the right wing, hares with it till he's smashed by a tackle from the visitors' full-back.

The 'hit' – it exacts an *'Oof!'* from the felled flyer – is brutal, but within the laws.

And, to a similar pattern, the game goes on. There *is* violence of a kind: in the collisions. And yet…

For all of the first forty, there isn't a punch, a butt, a stamp, or even any dissent. Far from fighting, the players help one another up from the floor. On those rare occasions when they are penalised, they surrender the ball (without protest), and retreat.

At half-time, coming off, he notices that the pitch has lost its sheen… that, in places, its surface has started to cut up.

But that is all.

***

In his changing room, tea is waiting – hot, malty and mud-coloured – in a big mug that may once have been white. The mug is chipped and has a black, spidering crack, but he appreciates the gesture. There are sugar lumps in small packs by its side.

Only when sipping, does he wonder about ingredients that might have been added: syrup of figs... creosote... weedkiller.

He imagines his poisoners' contempt: *Seen where this bastard's from? We'll teach him. Comin' up yer... bloody G-and-T-er!*

Yet he thinks the better of it – and drinks.

He massages his calves, which are tight, and he tells himself – again – that he's right to be finishing; that – come the weekends – there'll be 'other things'. A boat in the marina, perhaps.

He wonders now how many games he's reffed.

Five hundred? Sure to be. And no one gives a damn. Which is why he's bowing out, like this: a dead rubber that District couldn't cover... two teams who are going through the motions – if that.

He checks his watch, rises, makes for the door.

Forty minutes left... after twenty-five years.

At least the buggers are behaving.

***

The players are 'out': ready for him.

For a moment, he wonders if they even came in.

Their clusters remind him of the firs in the mist on the mountain.

He notices that the crowd now is bigger – *far* bigger: a proper cup-match crowd, a full-on derby following.

He thinks the stewards must have opened the gates – as sometimes happened – and let the locals in.

The sheds are stuffed with spectators. Above their heads and beneath the tin roofing: clouds of steam that again turn his mind to the mountain road. He'll take the valley route home, and no mistake.

The terraces seethe with supporters. At the sides of the pitch, youngsters hang over hoardings for Kylie's Café, Gwyn's Garage and Evans Bros, Monumental Masons.

This time there really is a roar as the half kicks off.

He senses a snarl among the players.

Yet the game continues without incident.

Except, it seems, when it comes to him.

He finds himself being caught by small nudges… shoves… collisions… even trips, that occur off the ball.

To begin with, these are followed by apologies – 'Sorry, ref!'… 'Didn't see you there, sir.'

But, after a while, they are not.

At one point, having been jostled by players from both sides, he goes down, on his arse, on the floor.

Laughter – and not laughter of the embarrassed kind but of the mocking, revelling-in-it, 'Look at him!' catcall kind – surges through the crowd.

One of the players – unsmiling and wordless – pulls him to his feet. Not a *helping* hand, it seems, but one proffered for the purpose of merely beginning the cycle all over again.

Wiping mud from his shorts, he notices – underfoot – how the pitch has deteriorated.

White lines barely visible, it's little more than a slurry patch now.

***

Midway through the half, he whistles for an infringement: a pile-up, centre-field.

The players dislocate from the steaming mound.

As they peel from it, he sees a face – buried at the bottom – that is familiar and grinning.

Billy 'Goat' Rees... Billy the Bastard... Wild Bill. A psychopathic flanker of the old school. List of convictions longer than any line-out: no part of an opponent's anatomy that he hadn't stamped, gouged or bitten. Carrier – some said – of a cut-throat razor in a secret pocket of his shorts, a screwdriver in one sock and a tungsten drill bit in the other. Banned *sine die* after multiple sendings-off. Three by him.

How the hell can he be down there? The man is dead, surely? Off the mountain, in his pick-up – full of beer and tears: a note safety-pinned to the front of his No 7 shirt... about how all he'd wanted was to play.

'Goat' – wild heath of hair, swine-eyed squint and a nose more busted than that of any old-time booth-boxer – rises from the ground... and winks. He walks off, melting into the morass of the other players.

They breathe hard, spit at the field, smear snot on their collars and their cuffs.

Their shirts, limbs and faces are caked with mud that has a tarry blackness. It is irrigated with oily channels that stream from them, like sewers.

The bigger men seem elephantine. It is as if they have emerged from a bog.

They study him with bloodshot, peephole eyes.

Although playing the game, its outcome to them seems of minor concern.

He begins to have the sense that – for all of their alleged rivalry – *playing… acting*, is what they're really about; that what they are engaged in is mere ritual, of a kind.

***

At times, amid the stinking shirts and filthy faces, he seems to see figures in much cleaner kit. Reserves, he presumes (though their 'coming on' is something that escapes him). As well as being almost unmarked, their shirts are different, older. No lurid ads or logos (*Delme for Diggers… Cheng's Chinese*). These men – who thread through the others in a way that is shadowy and marginal – are smaller, slighter… spirit-like.

It's as if they've climbed down from the frame of an old clubhouse photo: one of the kind in which the subjects – coalminers to a man – sit boyish and cross-legged; others of their number standing and staring, solemnly, away from the lens of the camera.

He tells himself that they can't be there… that it is all a trick… of the light… of the mist… of his mind.

They are wisps that have come down from the mountain… wisps that dance and drift.

***

Come the last quarter – never mind the mud and the thud of boot to ball – he and the players seem almost ghostly. They move, in an odd, self-contained silence, like figures in an old monochrome film.

There are moments of peculiar distraction. For one, although he knows they cannot be there, the faces of his mother and certain uncles – and great-uncles – appear in the crowd.

Meanwhile, the pitch has become little more than a mire. He feels the burden of dark clods that cling to his boots. For him, running is impossible now. He trails the play, like a lame, limping animal. At best, he walks, and even staggers.

He yearns to be away from there: this dead end, this graveyard, this tip at the top of the valley. The sea... the sea – that's what he wants to... see. Calamari at 'Carlo's', with the children... finished university now, getting jobs, doing well. And he will. He will. Just as soon as this fool's errand is done.

***

He notices that the crowd is thinning... almost back to how it was at the start.

Can hardly blame them. Not much of a game – for anyone. Least of all him: *All this way... to ref a bloody nil-nil. Some send-off!*

Voices come in echoey shards from the few spectators who remain: the die-hards... till even they turn their backs.

He hears the words of one: 'Come on. Let's leave them to it. We've seen enough.'

He thinks: *No one is interested in being here now – at the death.*

The last act plays out on the far side of the field. The cloaking mist has come down from the mountain. In its murk and the mire of the pitch, the figures of the combatants are no more than a blur.

The scrum closes over him... and binds.

Head to head. Shoulder to shoulder.

Within its black womb, he sees eyes.

Amber.

Slit.

Angel Face

Carys Shannon

Sian is the self-proclaimed boss now. She's two years older so when Mum died, she got dibs on the rules. It was Sian who said we have to brave the freezing fog to get a tree, even though it's eight o'clock on Christmas Eve. So here we are shivering, rubbing our gloved palms together and waiting for the heaters to stop blasting cold air onto our numb noses.

The windscreen clears, not that it makes much difference as we crawl along, the fog hugging tight to the road; anyone walking through the village invisible until a ruler's length, appearing like the looming shadow of death every few metres. My feet are freezing so I turn up the heater. Sian sighs and turns it back down. I fiddle with the radio until it buzzes onto a station. She slams her hand against the knob.

'Don't.'

Sian can't listen to music anymore. I know that. It's a shame because we've got this great Christmas tape of carols, just one, and we listen to it every year; we know the order of the songs and all the words. It'll be weird if we don't put it on, or maybe if we do.

It's been three months and I still dream of Mum waving at me from behind a window; through the back windscreen of the car in front; behind any kind of glass that I can't break through, even though I pound my fists and wake up sweating with the effort. The grief book says it's normal, which is annoying. I'd like to think she was delivering messages from beyond and now that idea is ruined. She probably would have sent them to Sian though, known as the more reliable of the two.

I look over at Sian, hands on the wheel, knuckles clenched and white. I wonder if it's annoying that everyone says how much she looks like her. It's true though, she got Mum's thick brown hair and caramel eyes. She even got her smile, not that I've seen more than a thin line pulled tight across her face lately. She glances at me.

'What?'

'Do you still think the man who delivers the coal is my dad?'

'Angel!'

She used to tell me that daily and it's disappointing she's sorry about it now. She's become so reasonable. I wish we could still scream at each other. The coalman was a better option than our real dad anyway.

'You're seventeen, Angel.' She sighs as if I've failed a test.

'Don't call me that.'

'It's your name.'

'No, it's not. My name is Amy.'

'Fine. It's *our* name for you, what's the difference?'

'I don't want it anymore.'

Her hands grasp at the wheel, and she turns the heater back on to full. A blast of hot air makes the car stuffy.

'You can't change it; Mum gave it to you.'

I've been trapped in this name forever and now I want out. Mum saw my curly blonde hair and proclaimed her child a celestial being without thinking of the consequences. People used to give her pictures of cherubs and angelic girls praying and she'd hang them in my room. Tens of chaste versions of me stared back all through my childhood. My blonde ringlets made people coo and worst of all, touch my hair as if I was some kind of bless-ed child. So, I became one. Chaste and good on the outside at least; my hair deciding the person I was going to be before I even got a look in. But things are different now. Sian has been forced into the role of mini mum, stashing her teen mags and fags away; starting to wear drab clothes and being polite to everyone. She's changed, so why can't I?

The figures on the pavement distort and morph amongst the thick blanket of mist outside. Sian indicates and pulls the car into Beynon's Garage. One pump, one woman serving, and zero chance of them still having a tree if you ask me. She must know that but we're like actors running lines while we wait for the star to show up. Except she won't – we buried her months ago.

Mrs Beynon creeps through the fog, feeling her way over to us with a small torch lodged between her teeth. A bit dramatic but it'll make a good story to tell her family over dinner. She leans down into the window, sees it's us and her face performs the sequence we're so used to now – a smile, a frown as the penny drops, then a flicker of something. What is it, embarrassment, pity, fear? Sian rolls down the window. It squeaks as she turns the lever; too slow for all of us but we've got our smiles pasted on.

'Oh girls…' Mrs Beynon goes to say something then stops. The fog has already dampened her hair and face, now her eyes mist over. 'It must be so awful. I just…' She shakes her head and looks into the distance.

This has been happening since the funeral. Sian is good at it. I'm not. She takes Mrs Beynon's arm and squeezes it. I scoff and look out the window. Why are we always supposed to make them feel better? Sian repeats Mum's annual words, almost exactly, as if some magic incantation of the usual will bring her back.

'I know it's so late, but we were just hoping you might have one tree left. A sorry one that no one else wanted?'

Mum loved the sorry-looking trees. I'm sure that's why we would set out so close to closing time. The dodgy leaners, the scraggers, the less tree and more three thin branches; we've had them all.

Mrs Beynon's face scrunches up and she starts to sob. Selfish. What's she got to cry about? She'll be home soon with her family singing carols.

'Oh, darlings, I'm sorry. We haven't even got one left. I should have remembered. I should have…' She trails off. Yes, she should. It's not like we don't do this every year. A rage seizes me in the stomach, and I reach over and push down on the middle of the steering wheel. The horn blasts. Mrs Beynon jumps up. Sian thumps my arm away. It stings but I shout out through the window,

'Have a lovely Christmas!'

Sian is already driving us away. She turns sharply through the fog without indicating.

'What the hell was that?' There she is. That's my sister. I hope we're going to have a really good screaming match.

'She's a hypocrite,' I declare. And she's in good company because there are a lot of hypocrites around after a person dies; criers like Mrs Beynon, false complimenters, and worst of all our father, who sent a Christmas card but not an invitation.

Sian slams her hands against the wheel, stops the car and presses her forehead to her palms. She takes deep gulps of air. A horn sounds behind us. I expect her to just sit up and carry on, but she doesn't. She knocks her head gently against her fingers. The horn behind is louder now, hazy headlights push a little closer.

We don't move.

There's a knock at the driver's window. She doesn't even look around. I clamber around her to wind the window down. The slowness isn't funny this time. An elderly man taps on the descending glass.

'You broken down?' He peers at Sian. I push her backwards and she takes her hands with her, covering her face. I lean on the wheel, careful not to push the horn. What do moments like this require? Sian isn't making any noise, not weeping or sobbing, just silent.

Perhaps this is the moment for *Sugar Magazine*'s, 'Make Him Go Wild for You' look? We've been practising at school ever since I stole Sian's teen mags from the stash she hid and used them to make everyone forget I was 'grieving'. The girls said I do it really well too; the thick curly blonde hair and green eyes adding an angelic tinge, so no one can call me a slag.

I give the man my best wide-eyed look. He seems confused. The article didn't cover elderly men, maybe he's not used to it anymore or it could give him a heart attack. I smile normally just in case.

'We're just having a rest. She needed a break.'

'You think this is funny? Stopping in the road, in this weather? It's dangerous, girl. Tell her to leave off messing me about.'

'We're not messing about. Our mother died.' This has become my best ammunition in life. Sian says I shouldn't do it, but I don't see why other people should get the sympathy and not us.

He steps back a little, then lowers himself back to the window.

'I'm sorry about that.' He thinks for a second. 'Perhaps she shouldn't be driving if she's in shock.'

Sian takes this moment to slam her hands down, revealing a face wet with tears.

'We need a bloody Christmas tree, alright?'

I snap into my seat, grateful that she's back in control. The man's face turns to disgust.

'I'm calling the police as soon as I get home. I don't know what your game is.'

Sian doesn't seem to notice him go. She leaves the window open and a wispy mist trickles through. Her face is pale and the effort to breathe slowly shows in her white knuckles and clenched jaw. She's never rude to people. All through the funeral and afterwards she greeted every visitor with a smile, nodded along with all their boring stories.

I think we do need a Christmas tree.

'Let's go up to the top garage, it's massive and they've got loads of trees.'

'Mum didn't like it.'

Her head dips with the failure of it. It seems unfair to me that we're trying oo hard to keep up appearances for someone who isn't even here anymore. We had months to prepare. It's not like it was a complete shock. Mum even bought us both a grief book so we'd know what to expect. In chapter three it did say that not crying could repress your emotions and they would come out later in unexpected situations. Thinking about it, I haven't seen Sian cry until now.

She swerves jaggedly, pulls over with a screech, then screams as if she is about to have a baby, covering her eyes and wailing for Mum. I don't move. Yes, I think this is what chapter three might have been talking about. Her breathing is ragged, snot falls from her nose and mixes in all the wetness on her face. She repeats, 'I can't do it,' over and over from whisper to scream. It starts to subside, but her body continues to jolt and tremble in the aftermath.

'Oh my god.' She whispers to herself. 'I'm out of control. I want to drive this car into a wall. If you weren't here, I'd do that.' She sucks air in and pushes it out slowly. 'Sorry, I just need a minute.'

I nod gratefully, happy to wait it out but she starts again. The whole thing from beginning to end, only this time her body shakes uncontrollably in the after quiet. She scrabbles for her bag, scuffling inside for something. Out come two white pills.

'What are those?'

'To calm down.'

'Where'd you get them?'

'At the hospital after… they gave them to me that night to help us sleep.'

'Us?' All I remember was the cloying grey tea in the grey sitting room where everyone spoke in hushed voices. No one said anything about pills. She looks at me.

'It was just to sleep. I didn't want you taking them.' She pops both tablets into her mouth and swallows. Is this suicide? Should I get her to cough them back up?

'Wake me up when Christmas is over,' she says then sobs again, swigging from a bottle of water that's been rolling around in the footwell for weeks. I'm about to go off on one because technically she has swallowed something that belonged to me, when she unclips her belt and climbs into the back seat.

'Sian?' My voice comes out small. Hers is a slurry mumble already.

'I just want to sleep, Angel. For a bit.'

She crawls onto the back seat amongst the discarded chocolate wrappers and curls into a ball. I stare at her for a moment, then take off my jacket and cover her legs with it. There's an old towel in the back from when Swift our dog was alive, so I smooth that over her too. She's already nearly asleep or pretending to be. One way to find out. I climb into the driver's seat and put the car in gear.

No reaction from the hump of clothes in the back.

The car is running, and I click the seat belt over me. Adjust the mirror just like in my lessons and off we go. It's not as difficult as I thought. I don't know why my instructor makes me practise over and over again on the abandoned industrial estate. This is easy. The car speeds along roads that are long empty. I flick the radio on.

I will get this tree.

Then I will carry it and her into the house. We will have a presence bigger than us in the room, a giver of light.

A blue flash behind us breaks my thoughts and I pull over slowly. I take in a long deep breath and start winding down the window in anticipation. As the figure of a policeman breaks through the mist I relax, it's Owen.

'Didn't know you'd passed your test.' He smiles in through the window and I switch the inner light on so we can see each other. Owen is like the boys in *Sugar Magazine*, floppy haired and always smiling. I'm glad to be caught. He squats down so his face is at my level. 'You got your licence done quick.' He catches sight of Sian in the back and his face changes to concern. 'She alright?'

I nod and this is the moment I give him *the look*, dipping my chin and staring up at him through wide eyes.

'She's so tired. It's been hard…' I smile and this time remember to bite the corner of my lip as I look at him. Bingo. I think he's blushing. He looks away.

'Well, I was going to breathalyse you, but that would be pointless. Not old enough, are you?'

I fix him with a stare and say, 'I can drive and smoke and…'

I do the smile again and lip biting. He stands up and taps the top of the car.

'Best get her home, then. Go slow in this weather.'

I drive off aglow like a recently decked tree. Life as an adult will be easy if this is all it takes. Smirking, I head towards the garage.

As I pull up the fog is so thick that I can barely see the way in. I drive as close as I can to the kiosk, but the lights are all off. Sian is out for the count, and I want her to wake up at home in our lounge all decorated with the biggest tree she's ever seen. I understand how she felt now. Responsible. And I want to make it okay for her.

I jump at the metallic crash of a shutter being pulled down. A man in a thick jacket and scarf jogs over to the car. He taps on the window and shakes his finger to say they're closed. I wind the window down with all my might.

'Wait, please.'

He turns, pauses for a second, then jogs back over, bending down to my level.

'I'm not a mechanic, love. If you've got a problem, you'll need to call someone.'

I switch the inner light on again and look up at him.

'I know you're closed but I really need a Christmas tree.'

He chuckles to himself.

'I'm not Father Christmas, love. Want to get home for my dinner. It's all locked up.'

'Can you unlock it?' I do *the look* and lip biting without thinking, as if it's already become a part of my new adult self. His face is hard to read; he gives me the same look I got from my uncle Harold at the funeral when he said, 'Face like an angel', then stared at my body with slight anger or disgust. I still don't know what it meant.

This man squats down beside the window and smiles. 'Now, you look as if you should be perched on top of a tree.'

Heat flushes my cheeks and my heart pounds. He has lines on his face and must be nearly forty. He stares at me, and I look away. I hear him rub his hands together with cold.

'Ah, go on then.'

I beam at him, radiant. He leans into the window and points to his cheek. There's a faint smell of cigarettes and pine. My stomach knots. I've never kissed a man I'm not related to before. But I really need this tree, and I've read the theory in Sian's magazines, so it should be easy. I turn towards him and lean out of the window. *Take things slowly to make yourself unforgettable,* the articles always say. My lips hover for a second over his skin, then I plant a kiss. The scratch of his stubble makes me reel back, heart racing.

He looks me right in the eye, spinning my stomach into knots, then points to his other cheek, not smiling this time. I don't want to be unforgettable to this man. Instead, I sit back down in the driver's seat and look straight ahead. His crotch is level with the window. There it is. The bulge that older girls talk about, straining against his jeans. He bends so his face bobs in front of mine and mocks pulling at his jumper as if he's hot, breathing out and laughing like it was a game. I study my hands on the wheel.

'Well, a tree was it, that you wanted?'

'Yes, a big one.'

'Open her up then.' He chuckles and cocks his head towards the boot. I flip the catch.

'Don't get out, it's freezing, take it from me.'

I smile at his chivalry and wait. Everything is okay. Perhaps Mum is watching over me after all. She can see Sian fast asleep on the back seat and knows that when she wakes up the tree will make her feel better. We'll put the carols tape on, and even though it's sad, we'll sing along with it just like before.

The smell of pine fills the car as he hefts a huge tree into the back. The boot slams shut, and I let out a deep breath. My hand trembles on the key as I start the car. The passenger door swings open, and he slides inside. In the light his skin shows up more weathered. He reaches over and turns off the engine, grabbing my hand.

'What's your name?'

I glance into the back hoping Sian will wake up and tell him to get lost. But nothing happens and he squeezes my hand tighter.

Ghost Songs, 1985

Eryl Samuel

Lloyd darts into an alleyway to escape the jostling mob in the street. He unzips his flies, leans his forehead against the wall and empties his bladder with a groan of relief. A broad dark stain of steaming piss slithers down the pebbledash and trickles into the crevices between the broken paving stones. He has no idea where it's all come from; he'd hardly drunk anything since they'd left Wales yesterday, other than a few swigs from a shared flagon of cider.

He'd spent the night with his three butties in a second-hand Ford Escort in a lay-by somewhere near Tamworth, the air thick with curry sauce and vinegar and stale farts. It had been hard to sleep in the confines of the back seat with Trev slumped against his shoulder, snoring wheezily like a creaking pit-shaft lift. He'd stuck his fingers in his ears and snuggled down under his donkey jacket; but whenever he shut his eyes, the events of the evening before haunted his thoughts. He was still awake when dawn broke and the engine started up again. They needed to complete the final leg of the journey before first shift began.

Lloyd rubs his eyes wearily and gazes at his dismal surroundings. An ugly black vine of graffiti crawls up the walls on either side of the lane, laden with swear words and swastikas. He gobs into the puddle of piss and turns away.

You'd think he would be used to this by now, but it's getting harder and harder with every week the strike drags on. He stinks of sweat and lack of sleep and, not for the first time, he wonders if it's all worth it, if there's any point them carrying on. All the long drives, the scrimping and saving, the hand-outs and soup kitchens. The anger and hatred. For what? To be able to walk through the village with his head held high when it's all over? To not be the one who finally breaks?

What he wouldn't do now for a bacon butty and a coffee and a smoke. But he'd had to give all these things up. When you rely on charity to feed your family, such luxuries can't be justified.

This is what he'd tried to explain to Rhys yesterday, before he'd left. He'd just wanted him to understand that they all had to make sacrifices at this time, including him. He didn't mean for it to become a fight. Maybe he'd been a bit blunt with the boy, but for God's sake, he's sixteen now, he should understand these things. He'd simply told Rhys to stop listening to that stupid mini-cassette thing they'd bought him for Christmas, get off his arse and help out around the house for a change. He may have used the words *useless* and *wimp*, but the boy needed to grow a pair and start acting like a man.

Rhys hadn't responded. He'd simply glared back at his father insolently, silent as a mannequin. This had enraged Lloyd even more and something snapped. He'd ripped the headphones from his son's head.

'All you do is sit around moping,' he'd shouted at his son, 'listening to your soppy songs while your mam and me are at the end of our tether, fighting like hell to keep our heads above water so that kids like you will have jobs to go to in the future.'

Rhys had curled his lip and sneered. 'I don't want to work down a fucking mine, thank you very much.'

'Mind your language, boy. And let me tell you, there's nothing wrong with coalmining. It's a damned good career.'

'Ha! That's working out well, isn't it?'

Lloyd wasn't going to take lip like that from anybody, especially not from his own son. He'd looked at him and despised what he saw. The quaffed hair and soft hands. The snarky attitude. They'd been far too easy on the boy. Too indulgent. He'd morphed into a self-centred epitome of everything they were fighting against. Into one of Thatcher's children. Lloyd had felt his hand tighten and scrunch into a fist. He would have hit him too, if Beth hadn't slapped the boy first.

'You don't deserve this,' said his mother, snatching the stupid Walkman from him.

Lloyd re-joins the crowd, who are heaving now against the ranks of police strung out across the street. They are in full voice:

'There's only one Arthur Scargill, one Arthur Scaaargill, there's only one Arthur Scaargill.'

Lloyd doesn't join in. Not this time.

Instead, he takes his son's Walkman from his pocket and screws the earphones deep into the wax of his ears so that he doesn't have to listen to that bloody dirge once again. Even his son's crappy music will be an improvement. He presses play and starts to listen. There's a miserable, droning voice singing something about being *human and needing to be loved, just like everybody else does.*

Bollocks to that!

He presses eject and inspects the cassette. There's something written on the label. It says, *Mix-tape for Rhys,* in neat, girlish writing. There's also a hand-drawn heart, coloured-in with red felt pen. Lloyd smirks. Rhys is a sly one, aye.

He flips the tape over, slots the cassette back in and presses play. There's a man, at least he thinks it's a man, singing in a ridiculously high-pitched voice. He pulls up his collar and strains to hear the lyrics, but all he can hear is someone repetitively screeching, *cry boy, cry boy, cry*. It's not Quo, but at least it has an up-tempo beat to take his mind off the bitter cold weather and the mindless chanting of the crowd as they wait for the scabs to be ushered through their ranks.

He lets the music wash over him, losing himself in the strange falsetto voice and songs reverberating through his ears. Some of the other pickets turn and give him funny looks. He scowls back at them, before realising that he's tapping his foot in rhythm with the beat. Sod them, he'll dance if he wants to.

At the end of the tape he rewinds it, to listen again from the start. He turns the volume up, but there's no music. There's just the muffled voice of a boy talking. The boy has a Welsh accent, but it's not his son's voice.

I've made this tape for you, Rhys. I know you're going through a tough time at home at the moment. Narrow valleys breed narrow minds you know, but one day, things will get better. This first track is for us, and for Smalltown boys everywhere.

As he listens to this anonymous, disembodied narrator, Lloyd has a sense of being totally alone. He's not in the frenzy of the picket line with his comrades and butties, he's in a vacuum, floating in a sea of spectral shadows. He's eavesdropping on Rhys's private life, listening to a boy that knows Rhys much better than his father does. He's still in a daze when the music starts again.

And then the lyrics hit him:

But the answers you seek will never be found at home,
The love that you need will never be found at home.

After they'd rowed yesterday, Rhys had come downstairs and pleaded for the Walkman back.

It was his, he'd said, *they'd given it to him. They had no right to take it.*

Lloyd wasn't backing down. He'd told Rhys that he and his mother had gone without and sold off family heirlooms in order to pay for it, so they had every right to do whatever they liked with it.

'You can keep the bloody Walkman,' Rhys had cried, 'just give me the tape back. You never paid for that.'

Lloyd had felt the muscles in his arms tensing once again. 'It will do you good to go without for a while,' he'd shouted, 'the way your mam and me have gone without these last nine months in order to give you everything you needed, so that you could get on with your studying. So you'll never have to work down the mines you despise so much. Now stop whining like a little poofter. I'm ashamed to call you my son, aye.'

He hadn't meant it to come out like that, but he was angry and tired. He felt betrayed.

'I don't care about your presents or your money,' Rhys had shouted back. 'There's only one thing I want from you, one thing I've ever wanted from you, and it's got nothing to do with money. But you never give it to me. Never! I'm sorry to be such a disappointment to you.'

And with that he'd left, slamming the front door behind him.

Rhys was right; Lloyd didn't understand. He hadn't tried to understand his son. But now, listening to these songs, he recalls what it feels like to be young and he grasps what it was his son wanted. What he needed from a father. He was only human, after all.

'I'm not ashamed of you,' he whispers, under his breath. 'I didn't mean what I said. I am proud of you. Proud that you're doing so well in school. Proud of the things the teachers say about you. Your weird stories and drawings. I'm glad that you're going to get the chance to go to college and make something of your life. To get away from all of this.'

From somewhere towards the front, Lloyd hears raised voices and yelling. Around him, the crowd are growing restless as they perceive action behind the police lines. But Lloyd isn't interested in the cause of the commotion ahead. He needs to talk to his son. Now. There are things he needs to say to him, before it's too late.

He sees a phone box on the other side of the road. He weaves his way through the heaving throng and pulls the door open. It smells of stale urine and someone has drawn a big cock on the phone in black felt-tip. Lloyd plunges his hand into his pocket and finds a single ten pence piece. He picks up the receiver and rings home. Beth will be out by now, but Rhys should be having his breakfast before school. If he came back, that is, after the row last night.

He listens impatiently to the rhythmic ringing of the dial tone. No one answers. He puts the receiver down and dials again. Outside he can hear the noise levels rising. The crowd surges. There's shouting and swearing and pushing and shoving. The coppers are banging their batons on their shields. The scabs must be coming through. He feels the phone box shudder. A contorted face is rammed up against the glass.

At last, someone picks up the receiver. Lloyd tries to put the money into the slot, but it won't go. He can hear a faint voice on the other end, but there's too much noise from outside to hear properly.

'Hello, Rhys?'

Lloyd attempts to force the money in, but still it won't go.

'Damn it!' he curses.

He rummages through his pockets for more change.

Suddenly, the door of the phone box is thrust open. Lloyd turns to see a copper in riot gear filling the doorway. His visor is up and he's grinning broadly.

'Thought you'd hide in here, did you?' says the copper in a flat home-county drawl. 'Nice try son, but next time, try somewhere without a glass wall.'

At last the money goes in.

'Rhys, is that you?'

'Phoning for reinforcements, are you mate? Well, I'm afraid you're too late, the cavalry aren't going to help you now, Taffy.'

The copper grabs Lloyd by the collar and yanks him from the phone box. Lloyd stumbles to the ground and the spare coin spills from his grasp and rolls across the tarmac. He stretches out a hand to retrieve the money but the copper's size eleven boot pins it firmly to the ground. Behind him, the discarded receiver swings limply from its coil, humming monotonously.

'Grovelling for a 10p coin, are we? Sad, ain't it?' says another copper. He pulls out a ten pound note and dangles it in front of Lloyd. 'Know what that is, Taffy? You gotta do a decent day's work to get that. Bit of grovelling for coal like you're paid to do rather than coming up here and making a nuisance of yourself where you're not wanted. Still, it means there's plenty of these for us, eh lads?' says the copper, waving the note at the ghoulish line of faceless figures spread across the street.

'Very generous of you to think of us,' says the first copper, playing to his audience. 'I suppose I'd better earn that money then, hadn't I, eh lads?' He kicks Lloyd hard in the stomach.

Lloyd curls up, winded. A sharp searing pain shoots across his ribs.

'Loads of dosh and job satisfaction too,' says the copper.

Lloyd tries to clamber to his knees, but a baton cracks him around the head, knocking the Walkman from his hands and sending him sprawling back to the ground.

'Resisting arrest, are we?'

Lloyd is disorientated and his head is stinging from the impact. From somewhere nearby he can hear a faint voice emanating from the headphones like a wailing phantom:

Run away, turn away, run away, turn away, run away.

Lloyd lunges for the device. He's not worried about himself, but this belongs to his son. To Rhys. Before he can get his fingers to it, the copper launches a kick at the Walkman and boots it hard across the road. The phantom in the machine goes quiet.

'Back of the net!' shouts the copper to his mates. 'Hoddle fires in a beauty – one-nil to the Met!' The coppers chuckle and jeer.

Lloyd scans the street desperately to see where it has gone, but his head is throbbing and his vision is blurred. He manages to locate the gadget lying in the middle of the road in time to see the hoof of a mounted police horse thump down on top of it, pummelling it into the ground.

'Oh dear, oh dear,' says the copper with a smirk. 'Still, cheap as chips to replace for any honest working man.'

The copper and his colleagues grab Lloyd's shoulders and drag him over to a van parked in one of the side streets.

In the road outside the phone box, all is quiet now. There is no chanting or shouting or swearing or singing. No more fighting or music. Only the battered carcass of a Walkman lying like carrion in the middle of the tarmac, its spilled intestines of cassette tape rippling silently in the breeze.

An Intervention

Matthew David Scott

Monday's dead. Jen goes through a stack of used porn DVDs. She'll file the discs and censor any covers before putting the empty cases out on the shop floor. She used to just wrap them in brown paper but has become a lot more creative since she began going to the classes Terri runs at the community centre. She grabs her tote bag from beneath the counter and takes out her craft knife, some tracing paper and a sheet of white-sparkle-glitter-card. She gets to work.

Khalid can smell burning. He carries his laptop one-handed and screen open. Jen sees him approach and holds up a DVD case upon which she has dressed the formerly naked cover-stars in Elvis-style jumpsuits.

'Very nice,' says Khalid.

He places his laptop on the counter and goes back to looking at the daily sales comparisons.

'By the way,' he says, 'Kevin's on fire again.'

Jen half-heartedly slaps down the case on the counter and squats to fetch the squirty bottle from beneath. It sits in a cobwebbed space with a dusty first aid kit, stacks of unused customer reward cards and a box full of CDs with 'Kevin's Pile' written on the side in felt-tip marker. She takes the squirty bottle and shoves her tote bag back in among the clutter, taking extra care to make sure her pills aren't visible. She stands.

'You okay to watch things while I put him out?' she says.

Khalid looks around the otherwise empty shop.

'I think I'll manage,' he says.

Jen had always wanted to work in a record shop. Her aunt, Sheila, used to have a stall on the market, and that had been Jen's specific dream – to work on the stall with Sheila all day and DJ at night. But Sheila got cancer. It was a type not worth attempting to treat so she sold her business and used the money to travel.

When she died, Sheila left Jen her personal record collection. Unfortunately, she also left her the bill for its storage. This is a bill Jen can no longer afford to pay given what she earns working here at the town's number one retailer of second-hand electronics, games, DVDs and an ever-shrinking music section; it is here, by the CD rack, that one of the regulars, Kevin, is on fire.

'Hiya, Kevin.'

Jen has known Kevin for a long time. He'd been quite a famous painter once, back when this town had quite a famous art school for him to teach at. Jen first met him at the jazz nights he used to put on, Sheila dragging Jen along to see players of great renown coming from all over to here – to this place – drawn just as much by Kevin's artistic reputation as they were for the high-quality opiates he could procure.

'Hiya, Jen.'

When Sheila died, Kevin had given Jen a painting he'd intended to leave to her aunt had he not unexpectedly outlived her. Jen sold it immediately. She bought some new headphones, decks, a laptop, and paid for two years of record storage up front. She's had to sell the decks. She has never told Kevin any of this. She wonders whether she should ask him if he has a few more paintings knocking about but, if he had, she guesses he wouldn't be in this state: bent over his walker, porridge-faced, smoke pouring from the pocket of a tatty black puffa jacket.

Jen holds up the squirty bottle and wiggles it. Kevin looks down at his side, raises his right hand in apology and then brings it down to slap at the smoking pocket. The thud is surprising given his skinny frame, and he needs to grab his walker for balance. When he's sure whatever was burning is extinguished, he backhands a lank, greying fringe across his forehead and smiles a smile that has been pilfered by many over his fifty-something years.

'Sorry about that,' he says. 'How's my pile looking?'

'Full,' Jen says. It's always full. He usually only spends when he's found a few new things to take up the space that would be left in the box. She wonders what he's got his eyes on down here and reckons it's the Pere Ubu stuff that came in last week. Then she is thinking about the storage unit, those plastic boxes, alphabetised.

'Is everything okay?' he asks.

That evening, the craft class is peaceful with the quiet concentration of the dozen or so women in attendance. Jen only started coming to support Terri, but look at her now: tongue between teeth, mind uncluttered as she slices tiny squares from sticky-mirror-card. Those teeth of hers are straight and white; her lips are pink and thin; her face is flat, broad and the colour of freshly dried plaster. Long dark hair is twisted up in a messy chignon, a lock here and there dyed pool-chalk-blue, her eyes a paler shade. She, like everyone else in the class, is making a decoration for a Christmas tree. Others work on designs that decry the commercialisation of the season or implore the elves to organise; Jen's is a disco ball.

'Anyone we know?' asks Terri. She's bigger than Jen, broad shoulders made to look even bigger in a chunky red cardigan. She is holding up a piece of tracing paper that had been poking out of Jen's tote bag; it is covered with the outlines of naked bodies in various sexual positions. Jen snatches the tracing paper back. She and Terri have known each other since they were eleven, slowly overlapping for twenty-one years, a steady eclipsing of each other's worst selves and a spotlighting of their best bits, all moving at a pace that would probably see them perfect human experience itself if they could live until they were two hundred. But both are only thirty-two, so Jen stuffs the tracing paper back into the tote bag and pushes some hair back behind an ear pierced with multiple small hoops. Terri knows better than to ask.

On the walk home, they take the east side of the river. Artificial light is everywhere: neon blues beneath the footbridge, huge primary-coloured squares patchworking the new shopping centre, all the lights still on in the coffee shop that has recently opened to serve the newly built flats that now line the river. Jen and Terri don't live in one of the flats; they rent a small terrace a left turn after this next bridge coming up, the one where the light disappears completely except for the phone screen illuminating Jen's face: there's a promoted post for a self-storage place, there's another for credit scores.

When they get to the house, Terri opens the door and both women leave their shoes in the hallway on Victorian tiles. Terri heads to the kitchen while Jen goes upstairs to the toilet. She sits on the cold seat, goes into her tote bag and takes out two pills. She necks them. She looks at her phone. When she thinks it's been long enough, she flushes the chain.

Monday again and November bright. On the footbridge, gulls perch on cables, arses to the sun as they doze through the various rhythms beaten out on the walkway. Jen is wearing her black beret – she always finds a strange confidence when things feel irretrievable. Debt collectors will be picking up Sheila's records from the storage centre on Wednesday if arrears aren't settled in full and, even if she somehow manages that, Jen will need to find another place to store them. But her phone zaps 'Lady Day and John Coltrane' into her headphones, and she smiles at the runners going nowhere in the massive window of Pure Gym. She goes into Boots for a sandwich. She goes to work.

'Bonjour!' Jen looks up from her phone and across the counter. It's Kevin. He's wearing a new coat. 'Sorry,' he says, and Jen twigs that he's apologising for the bad beret joke. 'I've come for my pile,' he tells her.

She bends down to get the box and puts it on the counter so he can start his usual routine of taking some out, putting some back, checking condition but –

'All of it,' he says, 'I'll take the lot.'

She scans the CDs into the till and tells him the total. She asks him if he wants to put his reward points towards his purchase today. He shakes his head, reaches into his jacket pocket and pulls out an envelope baleened with twenties. She almost tells him to not be flashing money like that around here but –

'Has there much new come in?' he says.

'A few bits you might like,' she says. 'Want me to go and grab some?'

'No, thanks,' he says, 'I've got some time to kill.'

At lunchtime, Jen plonks herself at Khalid's desk and eats egg mayonnaise on brown bread. Khalid opened all the windows in readiness but Jen doesn't feel the cold. She kicks back on the chair and stretches out her legs. The chair rolls as far as the filing cabinet. She plants her feet. Brown envelopes lined with bubble wrap spill out of a cross-hatched metal bin. She puffs out her cheeks and looks at the desk: the old computer chirrups and hums. The keyboard could do with a deep clean. A screensaver of a private joke bounces around the monitor and makes her smile. She spots the calendar, the one with a different photo of Khalid's baby daughter for each month, and she flips to her favourite photo: father and child on the teacups at the fair. He's holding his daughter tight and his face is one of joy and care, broad smile but slender, brown fingers gripping the kid tight. His daughter has both arms raised in the air and is laughing and— what is her name? Jen thinks. She can't remember, so she scoots herself back over to the desk and knocks the monitor alive with a shake of the mouse. She clicks opens the customer reward database and checks that Kevin gave her his real address.

Evening now, kids on bikes, the shush of their jackets and the slow tick-ticking as thick wheels waste time. It's a short street flanked on both sides by terraces of three-storey townhouses split into apartments: magnolia, black sills and frames, everything at right angles. Jen has seen this street hundreds of times walking up and down the hill as a child, and it has always struck her as beautiful and out of place. It makes sense that Kevin lives here.

She buzzes the number and waits for his voice. The lock clicks and she presses the tips of all four fingers against the door. It gives, and she enters a hallway with a high ceiling and a stone staircase.

Each step is tread-worn into a reverse camber, and she wonders how Kevin gets up and down them on his walker. She begins to feel a bit spooked. Terri would go mad about her putting herself in a situation like this without saying where she is, but she doesn't want to implicate her and, more than anything, is tired of Terri always having answers, plans, mitigation. Terri doesn't know about the final demands, unlike Kevin, who is already at his door when Jen reaches the third floor.

'Come in, come,' he says.

Jen takes a few steps into the hallway of the flat.

'Do you mind if I...' she crosses her legs and –

'Course, course, just there,' he says and points to a door at her right.

She locks the door behind her. She sits on the toilet seat. The bathroom is all white metro tiles. There's a Belfast sink and plump maroon towels form a ziggurat on top of a wicker hamper. The bath is free-standing but hasn't been adapted to help Kevin get in and out as Jen had expected. She opens up her tote bag and pops two clay-coloured pills from the packet. She thinks. She waits, flushes and leaves the bathroom.

She's about to turn left and straight out of the front door but she sees Kevin's new coat hanging from a peg on the back. She looks at the floor.

'I've just put the kettle on!'

It's him, shouting from beyond a sliding door at the end of the hallway – frosted glass in two panels. Jen walks towards his voice and then into a small antechamber. There is a kitchen to her left and the living room to her right. Is that a child's voice? she thinks.

'We've got the same tiles in our hallway,' she shouts.

'Take care of those,' he shouts back. 'They add real value to a place.'

They have definitely never spoken about property before. They have spoken about his discovery of speed as a youngster, and when he made his mother listen to *Metal Machine Music* with him after he'd shot up for the first time. They have spoken about how he snapped his back. She wonders what she is meant to be doing here. She heads into the living room.

Two butterscotch armchairs face each other across a small teak coffee table. In front of the chimney breast, a 90s hi-fi plays a CD – it's the child's voice. The alcoves are laddered with shelves of more CDs – no vinyl – and she thinks of the boxes full of the stuff in storage, the weird dystopian vibe of that place, how whenever she wandered past the individual storage units, she could only think of what it must be like to be locked inside. A large maroon rug. Parquet flooring. An ornate ceiling rose but a bare bulb. No paintings. She moves over to the window at the far side of the room. The streetlights begin to run like broken yolks.

'Sit down…'

She turns. Kevin has a tray. He takes tiny steps. Jen offers to help but she's cut off by a shake of his head. He places the tray on the coffee table and holds out his hand for her to sit in the chair closest. There is a small metal bowl and matching milk jug that look like they've been stolen from a hotel. The tea comes in white mugs. She picks one up in both hands and allows her eyes to track the heavy cornice that divides the white ceiling from the turquoise wall. There's a flute playing now.

'Roland Kirk,' he says. 'They lost his masters in a fire, you know? Lost a lot of people's work – real stars, real artists – but nobody knew for years, not until they wanted to re-issue their old stuff, wring a few more quid out of past glories only to find out it had all gone up in smoke.' He smiles. 'A bit rich, coming from me, I know.'

Jen watches the surface of her tea and the bright bulb throbbing there.

'It's a really lovely place you've got,' she says, trying not to sound too surprised. He smiles. She drums her fingers on the mug in sloppy time to the music.

'I've still got the studio over Crindau,' he says. 'When I stopped painting, it just became a place to keep everything I had left – finished pieces, unfinished pieces, the lot. I thought of burning it down once, for the insurance, but I knew that if I had that much cash in my hands at once I'd be dead in no time... My stuff can still fetch a few bob, believe it or not.' Jen's outline feels smudged but she keeps listening. 'I had my dealer come down the other day – art dealer, I mean – and when we got to the studio, he wanted it all or nothing; it wasn't worth his time taking any less. And I realised how little was actually left. The space itself was almost empty. It felt silly, a big place like that with nothing in it. And it was a peculiar feeling, too, like I'd been told how long I had left to live... I always wondered what I'd do, knowing that.' He shifts a little. 'She was an incredible woman, your aunt.' The words reach Jen like those bubbles you blow as a kid, taken by the wind, each one floating back toward her and bursting on her skin. She closes her eyes to save them from stinging.

'...the record company went through the catalogue of everything that had been destroyed and they prioritised those they thought they needed to find replacements for sharpish. Ella Fitzgerald was graded A as a priority. Louis Armstrong was graded A as a priority. The Pussycat Dolls were graded A as a priority. I don't know what they rated Roland Kirk. I've always loved him but I lost this album years ago.' Kevin stops speaking for a second or two to listen to the music. 'Of course, I could just go online and get this stuff but I can't remember what I've lost until I see it. That's what I've been doing in your shop – looking, remembering and slowly buying it all back.'

Jen keeps her eyes closed and begins to dream a happy ending to all this; perhaps one where she is in her early forties, actually in her own house or flat, bright walls and sun striping the floor through slatted blinds, no television, just shelves and shelves of music and a stereo system in front of the chimney breast; and even in this reverie she understands that she is simply picturing the room in which she is already sitting, just with added sunshine.

'I remember when you first started working there,' says Kevin. 'I remember because the music they played had become interesting.'

Jen feels his hand in hers. She opens her eyes and he is in front of her. He is floating a metre or so above the ground. And he takes the cup from her before it spills because she is floating too, rising from the chair so that both of them hover, positioned like skydivers in freefall. She looks at him and he smiles – it's catching.

Terri looks tired. Jen is at the dresser on a wooden chair. Terri is on the bed, back against the headboard. The sun is just starting to pink the bellies of a few clouds through the open window; it's freezing but Jen is applying sealant to her disco ball decoration.

'Can you drive a van?' she says.

Terri slides forward and leans back on straight arms.

'I drove that minibus to Green Man.'

She says it like a question.

Jen smiles.

'Shouting *fucking hippies* out of the window...'

They both laugh.

Terri stops.

'Why, you're not moving out, are you?'

Jen turns around so Terri can see her exaggerated eye-roll. She holds the disco ball up by its string and blows on it.

'No, I just need some of Sheila's things moving.'

'Hang on,' says Terri. She gets up and draws the curtains, switches the bedroom light off and takes out her phone. She turns on the torch and shines its light at the disco ball: the colours shatter about the room. Terri leans in close and taps the ball to make it spin. She whispers something. The first seagulls of the day have started gobbing off outside. Jen remembers the name of Khalid's daughter.

Fear and Trembling

Jonathan Page

His face is a withered oval fruit, his skin a pale grey. The Homburg lends him beauty, the blue suit, the polished shoes half buried in leaves. He does not belong to a wood in winter under a cloudless sky. He belongs in a yellow-lit, late night bar or restaurant.

The boy ducks but the man does not see him, only the car far below, a black box on rails of red mud. He recognises the regret that a job just begun induces, the way the man's lips part slightly, the way he removes and replaces his hat. He is just the same when his mother asks him to do chores. He is always stopping, when he knows he should move quickly and have done with it.

The man dips his head to the cupped lighter and when the cigarette is lit, throws back his head to inhale. The gunnysack must be heavy or the man is weak, unused to sustained physical labour. It has taken him a good quarter hour to get it even this far and his brow shines when he moves his head. The sack has ploughed a line in the leaf litter, a groove there, and then another, where there is mud beneath.

The copper town is full of bars. The boy has seen the men packed against the tall windows and the fights falling out of doors, men sprawling, staggering in a dance mid-street. The miners are a town to themselves and his Welsh father lives among them somewhere, though he no longer remembers his face. The musical voice remains, the boots that stood warming by the range. The sweet tobacco smell trapped in his mother's books, like butterflies or pressed flowers.

The boy decides the man is a poor man raised to a smart suit, that he is a citizen of the downtown, the once grand hotel on the hill where the women advertise themselves by combing their hair in lit windows. The sleek men in suits, the managers and engineers, leave their large houses in new cars and never touch the earth of the old city. This is what his mother says. This is how she divides the world and he is young enough to take her statement on trust.

The boy knows mean, though. School has taught him, fists in the yard. His gut is right not to help the man, only to watch, to see what he does and why. He followed in the hope of a few coins, of some gain, but there is something not right about a man in good clothes dragging a bag up a slope.

After the next war, the boy will read Kierkegaard. He will teach *Fear and Trembling* to steep halls of wealthy co-eds. The boy knows nothing of that future yet, but he sees how the same repeated actions – the man dragging his bag, stopping, smoking, going on again – can resurrect the settled question. Does he offer to help the man? His gut always says no, but for some reason he remains fixed on overriding it.

The man stops between two green rocks to lift the bag through the narrow way. As he does so, the boy sees black hair rise from its fabric. The man is as shocked as he is. He tips the bag over onto the level then wipes his hands fiercely on his pants. Once again he smokes. Once again, he looks back at the now invisible car.

The boy's mother works at a grocery store and takes in washing at weekends. She is always tired, a thin, blue-skinned woman with lank hair. Their house is a one-storey wooden box where the town turns to grass and sky. A grid of roads parcels the grass for some miles more, and at intervals collapsing signs announce the suburb that never was.

If he walks far enough he comes to the hills that ring the town. Sometimes he lies down under the trees to read a library book, or smoke a cigarette and simply listen to the wood. More often, he just keeps walking, deeper and deeper each time into the forest. For a space, he forgets the constant of his mother's sadness, which he takes for the eventual truth of all things.

It is not usual to find others in the woods. Nobody walks for leisure, and there is little game to shoot. A man in Sunday dress changes his worldview. The town was as distant as Mars before he saw him wrestling his sack off the road.

The man looks down from the cave mouth at a plain drained of colour. The polluted river is pure from up here, a snaking line that thickens in the turn as it enters the town. The boy has often stood where he has stood, looking down. The faintness of the picture makes him think of a cinema screen with the lights up.

Miners made these caves when the town was young. Rails still run from broken, laddered bridges up out of the trees. The caves are cool, roughly modelled halls. There is a pool in one with a white reflection suggesting depth that proves shallow up close. Beyond the pool is a chill, immaculate blackness that he has never entered.

The man takes off his jacket to reveal a holstered pistol. The sack sits against a rock to watch with him over the valley.

In five years, the boy will be able to strip, rebuild, load and fire his rifle in less than a minute. In twenty, he will march against the bomb, in thirty, against Vietnam. But on this hillside there is a glamour to a gun in its beautiful leather nest, the straps that puff the man's brilliant white shirt. The distant world of the movies, of gangsters and G-men, has proved its truth to him. Sense says slide down the slope and run. Get to the road, to other people as quick as you can. Then one wonder is trumped by another.

The man sings 'Men of Harlech' in a strong, warm baritone that belies his narrowness of frame. He closes his eyes, and turns the palms of his hands outwards, so intensely focussed is he on his song.

Men of Harlech, march to glory,
Victory is hov'ring o'er ye,
Bright-eyed freedom stands before ye,
Hear ye not her call?

The boy half rises, because he should go, and because the man sings so well. The man walks a small circle on the stony platform, smiling as he sings. It is hard to say if he is genuinely joyful or only letting off steam. The man breaks off mid-phrase.

Jesus, what…

The fourth wall is broken. The boy watches unmoving as the man fumbles with his holster. Only when the pistol is pointing at him does the boy turn to jump away. He sees the privacy of the pinewood below him, the short stair of mud by which he came. Fear is like pleasure. Then a stone slips out from under his mud-caked shoe and he slips onto his backside. It is comic, inevitable as a dream that he should fail. He hears the click of the hammer and pulls his legs up to his chest.

Get up here. Stand the hell up. Look at me.

The boy is calm, intensely present. He will remember the exact scatter of the rocks and the tracks barely exposed above the dirt and the sway-like breathing of the trees over the erased valley all his days.

Look at me.

It is hard to look at him, the sun is at the man's back, and the gun says look at the gun. It twitches its snub nose, rises and falls, with a balloon's impatience to escape. There is the man's small face, if he squints, the red shine of effort. Black hairs escape from his cuffs to form arrows on the back of his hands. He walks a slow circle to see the man's face more clearly.

Quit moving about. I'll shoot, you little shit. I will.

The violent words are spoken so softly that he stops to hear them. The man removes his hat, and forgetting the gun in his hand, wipes his forehead.

What you doin' here? Who sent ya?

Nobody, mister. I was walking.

In the woods, alone. You was walkin'. And you followed me, yes? So who sent ya?

Nobody, sir.

Walkin'. Why was you walkin'?

I like walking in the woods.

You like walkin'. Greaves sent you, you're spyin' on me.

Who's Greaves?

Who's Greaves, who's Greaves, he says... I should kill you. What did you see?

A man with a sack.

A man with a sack, I like that. I like that. You like a bullet?

I don't want no trouble.

You got trouble.

I don't want no trouble.

You say that, kid, and I say you got trouble. What did Greaves say?

I don't know no Greaves.

Sure you know Greaves. I can see you knows him.

I was walking, that's all.

Course you was walkin'.

They find what to say in the saying of it, thinks the boy. It is the same when he recites a memorised poem in class, there is nothing to say until he says it, and even when he says it, there is music, not meaning. The meaning sticks to the inside of the poem like honey to a jar.

You listening, kid? You drag the sack. Greaves sent ya all this way, you can do some work. Then I kill ya.

Okay.

Like you got a choice.

Close up, the gunnysack looks too small for a body, but it is heavy, and there is the iron scent of meat as he leans back on his thighs. The boy is proud of his new muscles, the height he has gained in half a year, and he is ashamed when the sack barely moves. Some part of him wants to impress the gangster. He tries again and the bag starts to move. He moves as quickly as he can towards the cave, without stopping, because it would be harder to start over if he stopped. It does not occur to him to take it slow, to put off the probable moment of his death.

Left here. Left…. Keep going… Go on.

Then there is the cold, high house of the cave, and the day sheered to whiteness by the transition. The rocks float on their shadows. The boy twists about to negotiate the steep smooth way to the cave floor. The rusted curls of the severed rails have always attracted him, and he pauses, without thinking, to contemplate their caught movement.

Right. Stop there, son.

As if he had not already stopped. In front of them, the floor shelves into immaculate darkness. To their right are lit courtyards, the pool in its near circular room. The man holds his lighter out to the darkness.

Greaves said find the tunnel. There's a tunnel straight ahead. Keep to a line he said. Is there a tunnel?

What?

What, he says, like he's dumb or something. Is there a tunnel?

The dialogue is from some movie, the voice Welsh. The cave draws out its song and lets the words continue beyond themselves, into the music beneath them. The boy is no longer curious about the sack he pulls, there is only the cave mouth and the darkness he sinks into. The sack rolls onto his foot, a dead weight, a skull maybe by the feel as he shifts his foot to free it. The man displays himself in orange flashes, his face, his chest, and the hand that holds the lighter.

Stop here. Stop, okay?

Okay.

What's your name, boy?

Jones, sir.

Jones, sir. Half the town is Jones. I am Jones. Your Christian name then?

David.

A third of the town. Your mam, what is her name?

Mabel. Mabel Jones, nee Horowitz.

That narrows it down. Yes it does.

You know her, sir?

I didn't say that.

He sees his mother flop the damp sheet over the line then pull it first one way and then a little the other so that it hangs correctly. Her hands are clever and her golden wrists glisten. The sheets swell and swing up on windy days and sometimes, rarely, they fall to the ground. There is hardly a mark on them but it breaks her spirit to see it. She may take herself off to bed, or else start the boiling and starching and mangling all over again, mixing perfectly clean sheets with the impure and fallen. But that is a rare occurrence. While the street of white sheets stands, she seems happy to him, and he is happy because of it.

Why this vision now and not another, he does not know. Maybe the man's white shirt in the charcoal cave.

So you'd be fourteen then.

Fifteen in June.

Near enough a man.

Mam wants me to work next year.

In a shop I bet, an office. Somethin' soft and brainy.

I expect so. She worries about money.

The boy does not understand the small talk. He is either about to die or the man is filling time while his eyes adjust. The man is a grey photograph and his voice echoes, almost speaks over itself, in the cave roof.

There it is. There's the tunnel. Stay here and do not move. I can tell if you do and then you're dead meat.

I won't move.

Better not.

The man motions the boy to let go of the sack. A perfectly black archway floats on the finer charcoal of the cave below them.

Let go then. Unless you want to join the sack down there.

Sorry, sir.

Mabel, you said.

Yes.

Think of your mam. No moving.

The man vanishes into the tunnel but the shuffling sound of the sack and the man's effortful breathing are audible for some time. Eventually he hears only the blood in his ears, his own breath.

The boy imagines running to the cave mouth, the shot filling the hall. He falls from the bitten rails or else shivers to his knees where the bright ground begins. Saturday morning serials, Westerns, have shown him how to die. He is cold and profoundly tired. He would like to lie down and doze but that too feels like a violation of the rule. All in all, he is a good boy and does as his elders tell him.

He does not know how long he waits. Five minutes, fifteen, who knows? He wonders if the man has taken another way out of the cave or has had some kind of accident.

When he opens his eyes, he sees a small perfect picture of the man inside the tunnel. There is a bluish halo about the lighter and he can make out the man's hat, the collar of his shirt. The picture blinks out and thirty seconds later reappears, only slightly larger. The boy panics for the first time. Death has come at last.

See, they now are flying!
Dead are heap'd with dying!
Over might hath triumph'd right,
Our land to foes denying...

The cave makes a better singer of the boy than he is. He repeats the same few lines over and over because he struggles to recall more. He falls silent then roars 'Men of Harlech!', that phrase alone, as if the song continued on without him, a cave river, erupting into sight at intervals.

The Saxon's courage breaking!

He hears the lighter and the man is before him, his gun levelled.

You will never make a singer now will you, David? Not singing like that.

I would like to learn.

It is not in you, boy, I can tell. I have an ear for these things. Now close your eyes, will you?

David does as he is told.

Are they closed?

Yes.

Good.

He hears the man cock his gun. He shuffles his feet into a wider stance and holds his breath against the blow. It is not fair for the man to play with him like this. Shoot, get it over with. Shoot me. The next thing he hears is a pebble skating over the cave floor. The man is far away, climbing to the rails. He notes the cross stroke of his hat as the light enfolds him.

Keep your mouth shut, boy. I know who your mam is, remember.

I know… I know, Dad.

So you guessed the same. You guessed. Clever lad. You'd get that from your mam. She was always the clever one, always reading she was.

What will you do to us?

Nothin'. I won't do nothin' unless you talk. No telling now. Tell Greaves if he asks but nobody else.

I don't know who Greaves is.

So you say. Tell him anyway. He don't take no for an answer.

David will wonder for the rest of his days if he misremembered or even made up their final exchange. There was a strong possibility the man said nothing, only holstered his gun and left him be.

He drinks from the cave pool because he is too thirsty to care if it is poisoned, and after sitting on the rails for a while, walks home. He comes to the tambourine shake of the wire fences on the plain that fenced nothing, then the white matchbox houses in their orange haze. The asphalt is still hot when he reaches it, and his body hollow, elevated, as if he had a fever. When his mother opens the door to him she does not ask where he has been because he is often late home and besides, almost grown. She puts soup and bread on the table and tells him to wash afterwards because he stinks. The criticism is enough to make him cry, and he would have told her the whole truth then if she'd asked, but she did not ask.

To protect his mother, he kept his word about the sack until his return from Germany. The police found nothing in the old mine workings but treated him kindly nevertheless, knowing the trauma that war inflicts upon a man. He never found his father, despite hiring a PI in the early fifties. It was easier for a man to disappear back then, to change names, identities. The whole problem of it, the transference of filial love to a violent stranger, was what drove him in part to study philosophy and write books on duty and the will.

As to the man's singing, his mother was adamant his real father could not hold a note to save his life. That proved nothing though – he was a strong believer in buried talent and the ability to learn new skills. The year Stanford granted him tenure, he became a stalwart of the university's male voice choir.

My How To Guide

Satterday Shaw

1. Run For Your Life.

Barricade yourself in your room. It's not even your room, which you've never had your own room because you used to share with Wayne when your mum did it up with Winnie-the-Pooh wallpaper and bunk beds. The small back room with the chipped wardrobe the colour of bitter chocolate where we kept our coats in summer. A funny smell creeps out from the mothballs and hovers round me till the kids at school say, 'You stink like my dead granny.' Naphthalene, they call that chemical, and they make it out of coal tar. I picture Naphthalene as a beautiful girl who has everything perfect, black hair that fans out round her shoulders when she flicks her head, a voice that's posh but not snooty, 34B boobs so she can buy a bra in Primark or Top Shop and it fits.

I shove the chest of drawers against the door because I can't shift the wardrobe on my own. On top I pile library books, the rubbish bin, my shoes. Not to make it harder for somebody to get in but so I'll wake up with the clatter of it tumbling off. Build it like Robinson Crusoe building a shelter under waving palm trees, wondering if he'll stay lonesome until the end of time. I want somebody, a dog called Friday who'll lick my nose and wag her tail.

No ships on the horizon? Lash yourself a raft, push it out,

jump on. Pack your mum's old suitcase, though it doesn't even have wheels, wait till Dad and Wayne have left and drag the case down the lane across melting tarmac to the stop on the opposite side of the road from the one for school. Say goodbye to pigs and cowpats. White flowers so fragile one gust of wind can blast their petals away. If any nosy old bag asks if you're off on holiday, say, 'No, just sorting clutter.' Guessing you're getting rid of your mum's stuff, she'll shut up.

2. Don't Talk to Strangers.

On the bus I stare in a daze at the backs of old blokes' ears like sausages, cooked, raw, flaky, peppered with blackheads. Dead grass and dried mud. We slow to a rattle behind a combine harvester in between fields. Somewhere to live is the most important thing, then A levels, a Golden Retriever puppy like in the Andrex ads.

As we pull into the bus station, I balance to the front to make sure nobody gets off with my case. It bangs against my legs as I wrestle it through the automatic doors.

'Let me give you a hand with your bag.'

He's older than me but not too old, like thirty or something, wearing clean jeans, and trainers which would fetch serious respect in high school.

'No, I'm fine,' I say. Strangers shove past me with bags of shopping, mothers and daughters, couples. Huge glass windows cage us away from the roar and stink of buses.

'I can't watch a young lady struggling. Here, if you take my phone, you'll be sure I won't disappear,' he says.

So, when he presses this mini, matt-black Samsung into my palm, I let him heft my suitcase. He's so well spoken, not like most blokes. In my grubby tracksuit, with hair I haven't washed for a week, I'm not feeling my best.

'Where to?'

'Oh, I don't, I'm —' Try not to stutter, falling through empty space like a snowflake in August.

'I'm Tray.'

'Aretha.'

'What a lovely name.' One of his eyes is brown, the other blue.

3. Make Friends with Girls in the Same Boat.

I tip three heaped teaspoons of chocolate, add real milk not the semi-skimmed stuff, into the microwave, thunk. Click Play on the cassette machine, Chain of Fools at the start sounds a bit weird like foreign music where the tape has stretched but I can buy a CD soon as I get a CD player.

Light through the sycamore tree strokes the wall. Two coats of Calico. The leaves have started to turn brown and curl in on themselves. I use a tea-towel to take the mug out of the microwave, pick up my new phone and flip it open. The battery shows green, screensaver a snap of Tray, smiling.

I jump when the buzzer rasps, lean out the window. Tray's face makes me want to flutter down to him through the sunshine. Instead I chuck the key down in a plastic bag.

He walks in with some girl I've never seen before. 'This is Maxine.'

I can't even look at her.

'The place looks nice, babes. You always keep your place nice.'

'D'you want a cup of tea? Or coffee?' I hover near the kettle. Tray doesn't like hot chocolate and I'm certainly not going to use up milk on Maxine. My hands shake as I shove the plug in.

'I know you girls love make-overs and shopping, so I'll

leave you to get on with it.' Tray jangles his keyring round his index finger.

All of a sudden, he's so close all the hairs on my arms stand on end and I can smell this different, oaty smell. It breathes off his neck under his usual fabric conditioner and aftershave. His lips feel warm and soft as a puppy's skin. The first time he's kissed me. He knows how I'm feeling. He didn't kiss Maxine. He's out the door.

Older than me, twenties maybe, short, straight black hair, stiff like dolls' hair. She has milk and two sugars in her coffee, dips a couple of Custard Creams.

'He wants me to shape your eyebrows. Okay with you?'

I nod. 'Sorry I haven't got Internet or satellite. You can't even get all the Freeview channels here.'

'I like the music,' she says.

'It's my mum's tape. That's why I'm called Aretha.' But I put the telly on when it gets to the end of the side.

While a repeat of *Without a Trace* jabbers away, Maxine tugs stray hairs from under my brows. I try not to flinch. A wrinkle shaped like a rainbow across the bridge of her nose makes her look as if she laughs all the while. She smells of cigarettes and marzipan.

'Is he your boyfriend?' I dare to ask. On telly this gorgeous Golden Retriever is snuffling a scent down a dark alley.

'No. No way he'd —'

But that's all she says about Tray.

4. Don't Fall In.
He kisses and strokes me like a May breeze kissing lilac blossom, like a bee burrowing into a flower. Not quick and stinky like farm beasts, not like before. I'm dripping when he slides inside me so it doesn't even hurt. I lie awake all night,

listening to him breathe, breathing his CK cologne and that porridge smell of his skin together with sweat like mould on satsumas. At work all day I burn. When I get home, touch myself with my fingers till I do something like a sneeze inside, like a fit of giggles or tears, like doing a poo when you're dying to go. I want more.

5. Stand Up for Yourself.
'You have to swallow the smoke, babes, suck it down into your lungs,' he says.

Better than fags in the alley down the back of the Science Block, doesn't make me vomit. Coughing and choking, I wash it down with my red Breezer. Even when I've passed the spliff to Tray, my breath still puffs smoky on the black air. My heels make me stumble inside through the fire door. I can't dance in heels. Red tinsel and balls shine above the bar. The music turns liquid, pours through the air like Golden Syrup, stirs round my bits turning me into a hot magnet till I want to rub against him. He can't stay away from me, either. Stink of beer makes me think of Dad. Don't. I squeeze past the men's eyes, grabs on cranes that lift me through the dark in metal teeth. Women's eyes like the school canteen. I wiggle my fingers at Maxine on the dance floor. Look, I'm with Tray. Though I'm dying to kiss him, my mouth has dried up so I've got to swallow more Bacardi Breezer.

Tugging me down the corridor past the toilets and the fruit machines, he pulls me against him until his eyes blur together. His lips against mine dissolve me into hot, sweet and milky, not separate any more.

'Here.' His mouth tickles my ear.

'No.' I try to wriggle away from him. 'Somebody might see.'

'If you loved me, you'd do it,' he says. Or, 'It would make

me feel so good. I'd do anything for you, babes, but you won't even do this one small thing for me. Aren't you worried I'll go off with somebody else, if you don't do me what I like?'

Do it in the club. Take it up the bum. Let him handcuff you. Take photos of your down-there.

6. Look Out for Number One.

'I wondered if you could help me out, darlin'?' he says, leaning back against the cushions on my bed.

'What d'you mean?' I run the cold tap before I fill the kettle.

'You know I have to pay out to my ex-wife and kids. It's not cheap, taking you out, or when I bring you round some Malibu or a little spliff. And presents… your phone, like that.'

He always told me not to worry. I spoon coffee granules into a poodle mug and a spaniel mug, add sugar. As I turn to listen to him, rain splatters the window. Outside, the storm trembles new green leaves on the sycamore. I'm a country girl at heart but now I live in the town.

'I'm in a bit of trouble. This bloke I owe some money to, he's seen you. If you just spend the evening with him, he'll write off what I owe him.'

'How much? You can have my savings, for college.' When I turn away, pores open on my face from the kettle boiling.

'More than a grand.'

It hits me like Dad's fist. I turn back.

Tray smiles. Lovely, white, regular teeth. 'See how much he likes you, babes? One evening. You know you're mine. Me and you, I think we should have a baby.'

I miss the mug, scald my hand. 'I don't want a baby. I want a puppy,' I say once I've got the cold tap gushing over the burn.

'I'm allergic to dogs,' he says.

7. Don't Have Kids Unless They Can Swim.

Water sloshing down the pavement freezes my toes. My shoes slam the balls of my feet against the tarmac. Rain shivers rear lights into red smears. I could do with a nice, warm pair of trainers, Skechers maybe like Britney used to wear. Tray would go berserk if I wore trainers to work. Ladies in China used to have their feet bent double into pigs' trotters so they tottered around on points like ballerinas which was supposed to be sexy. I wouldn't let anybody fold Tanya's feet.

A Freelander swishes past, sending up a wave. A Golden Lab stares out the back, from behind bars.

My fingers clamp round the handle of my brolly. I wedge the bottle into that hand while I unscrew the cap. I always swore I wouldn't drink every day, not like Dad, end up with a purple nose doing stuff I was sorry for next morning. It's supposed to be undetectable but it smells sour, like the rain. I swill it round my teeth and tongue to wash away the bitter taste of the condom.

Thank feck for my stupid silver plastic mac even if it doesn't keep the cold out. Last time I wore this mac, this effing copper drove me right up Birchgrove and left me there. I walked back with blisters oozing on my heels and toes. The river's roaring. You see people's houses on the News, ruined. Imagine all the shit backing up the sewers, the place would stink. I can't swim even though Dad used to swing me by an arm and a leg and chuck me in the deep end. If Tanya ever fell in the water I couldn't save her. A Golden Retriever would jump in, all four feet together, grab Tanya's belt in its gentle mouth and paddle back to shore. Like in the Lassie movies on the box. 'Dad, can we get a puppy? Please?' About as likely as Tray driving up now and when I get in he says, 'Reeth, I love you. Let's get married.' I need to have a serious talk with him.

The wind chucks a white pulp against my leg. Not a chip paper. REWARD, it says, with a photo of a spaniel's head with a little kid's arm round its neck, the rest of the kid cut off. Answers to the name of King. Phone number.

A Mondeo pulls over. As the window glides down, the white-haired stranger at the wheel asks, 'How much for a blow-job, love?'

When Tray's old Beemer splashes in to the kerb, I step across the torrent in the gutter to fall onto the passenger seat.

'You look like a drowned rat.' He passes me a ciggie from the gold pack. I hand him the notes I've kept dry down my bra.

'I need a bit extra.' I suck the flame up my fag. A wisp of hair sizzles. 'We're gonna get a puppy, me and Tans.'

'That's not going to happen, darlin'.' He's smiling. He always smiles. Headlights pat the back of his head but his face stays in the dark so that both his eyes look the same colour. He always smells clean, fabric conditioner, Calvin Klein. The last punter I did smelled like mushrooms, like a fox. I picture our daughter rolling in a field, laughing, romping with a puppy, sunlight through her curls. I chew my lip, the place where it's already sore.

'Anyway,' he says, 'it would be cruel. You haven't got a garden.'

I don't say anything else, just run a comb through my hair before I tip back out in the rain. I'm about to call it a night, pick Tanya up from Maxine's or sleep on the settee round hers, when this Vauxhall Astra toots at me.

'I been driving round, looking for you.' He's a nice old fellow, a regular.

My heart wriggles. 'You got it, then?'

He's sleeping on the back seat, in a rug. Reaching for him, I cuddle him in my arms, sniffing his scent of meaty biscuits, a warm, clean smell like babies. Tans is going to love him.

8. Set Your Daughter a Good Example.

The puppy squeals when Tanya grabs his ear.

'Gently, babes.' I gently straighten her fingers into a chubby starfish and show her how to stroke his head. Wagging his tail, he squirms, all warm and fat. His fur seems a bit short for a Golden Retriever but maybe it'll grow. I yawn. Tanya falls on her bottom with a thump. The puppy trips over her legs. They make me laugh.

'What shall we call the doggy?'

'Goggy,' says Tans.

'Snoop Goggy? No, I mean a name, like you're Tanya, and I'm Mummy, or Aretha.'

'Mummy,' says Tanya. Then she goes off into a long burble which I can't understand.

My Aretha CD is playing in the background. 'How about Rock Steady? Rocky for short,' I say.

Lucky Rocky has collapsed in a Beanie-Baby ball when I hear Tray's feet. By the time his key rasps in the lock I've scooped the puppy into his lemonade box and pushed it under the bed.

'Daddy,' says Tanya. She stretches her arms up.

While he's sitting her on his knee, I shove the saucer of food and the bowl of water into the cupboard under the sink.

'D'you want a drink?' I ask.

'Make me a coffee, darlin'.'

'You look cute in your little warm-up suit,' he says when I take Tanya off him.

She's falling asleep so I pop her in her old cot she's too big for and fetch him the coffee. He lights a cigarette. I wonder how long puppies nap.

'We need to talk.' I pull the armchair opposite the bed where I can see Rocky if he rolls out under Tray's feet.

He flinches away, teasing me. 'Sounds serious.'

'You lied to me.' It's his left eye that's blue. Tanya takes after his right eye. 'I don't mean about your wife and kids. I mean about the A levels. I checked with the college. You don't even have to pay fees to do A levels. I could have got a maintenance grant.' Maxine told me. A faint whine sounds from under the bed. 'That's what you don't understand, Tray. You thought if I had a baby I'd be chained to you. But I'm tied to my girl, not even like there's any knots but we'll always be part of each other. I want to set her a good example.'

His face drips rainy with sweat while his breath grates in and out. Another whine. Tray strides around the crowded room. Opens the wardrobe, the drawers. Finally, he kneels and pulls out Rocky's box.

With the puppy yelping in one hand, he runs both taps to fill the sink.

'Tray. Don't.'

Still scraping for breath, he plunges Rocky into the sink full of water. That's not how it's supposed to be.

'Please.' I tug at his arm but it's hard as a tree trunk. He doesn't look at me or hit me or anything.

Hearing Tanya sigh, I hurry across to the cot. She's still asleep although she's pushed the cover off. Feeling if she's warm enough, I hold her bare foot for a minute, soft and solid, it fills the palm of my hand, each toenail perfect, delicate as the petal of a flower that a strong wind could destroy with one gust. Her second toe is the longest, exactly like mine only miniature. As she kicks against my fingers without waking up, I remember her kicking the inside of my belly before she was born.

9. How To Get Rid of a Pimp.

That's not what I meant to write, at all. The teacher on my Access course said, 'Use any style,' and when we asked what she meant, she said, 'Like a letter, or a newspaper report, or a story.' Mine was going to be an article for a magazine: 'How 2 Get Rid of a Pimp,' like 'How 2 Zap Your Pimples' or something. I did it on the computer at college while Tanya was at school, easier than on my phone. In February she's going to start full time. It's my main piece of work for the term and I spent weeks writing it. I wrote in the present tense like it's happening to me now. Like I'm doing it now. I used the spellcheck all the time and read it out loud to myself so it would sound like me talking. The tutor said because I read a lot, that'll help with my writing. Except it's come out more like a guide of what not to do, a bit of a failure. I know there are parts I've skated over because I need to hang onto my pride. I expect I'll have to do it all over again, but I'll show my tutor first.

The Space Between Pauses

Bethan James

I run my fingers down the curtain seams: they feel bumpy like the stitches down my chest. Perched on my bedroom windowsill, I wait for her to appear down the lane. Everything is green as if an artist's palette ran out of all the other colours. My village in Wales is surrounded by fields and forests and bracken-ringed clearings that she told me are fairy circles for the Tylwyth Teg. Even the silence is green. I was wearing my green corduroy dress when the accident happened.

Something moves in the corner of my eye. Rhys from school is shooting at swallows in next door's garden again. A water pistol rests in one hand, as a strawberry ice cream melts under sticky July sunshine in the other. He aims high in the sky then fires pop shots. I wave, my arm heavy in its bone-white plaster cast. He carries on gunning down birds.

Not that I'm bothered or anything, because Gran's visiting today. My mamgu. She smokes rolled-up cigarettes, dyes the tips of her hair indigo, and even has a tattoo swimming across her shoulder. I thought it was a dolphin, but Gran said no, Cerys. Wrong species. Clue's in the face: porpoises are the ones born with a grin.

Her motorbike roars onto the driveway and petrol fumes force their way through my bedroom window. Once, I overheard

Dad say she's more "forse mashure" than mother-in-law, whatever that means.

I head downstairs. I haven't had many visitors since I was let out of hospital. Maybe people from my class are away on summer holidays? I pluck at a loose thread on my sleeve. I'm wearing my lucky jumper today. It's sea-foam green. When I walk it sways like a wave swell and I imagine I can taste salty spray. Good things happen when I wear this jumper, like the time Mum told me my art homework was wonderful and patted me on the shoulder. Mamgu visiting is a good thing. But I can't wear my lucky jumper too much or I'll wear the luck out with it.

Anyway, Gran's here because Dad's out at the village barbecue down the green. He says the other children at the get-together will be too rowdy – 'It could set back your recovery, Cerys.' Safer for me to stay inside for the school holidays after the operation. Mum's still in her shed finishing a painting. I saw the canvas through the window yesterday. It was big and red and full of jagged lines.

Gran's already in the kitchen helping herself to warm bara brith cake speckled with raisins by the time I make it downstairs on my crutches. Her motorbike helmet sits in the middle of the table like a severed head. She gives me a big hug. It hurts but I don't care. Hair the shade of a freshly polished knife hangs down her back.

'Prynhawn da. And how's my little cariad?' Gran says, wiping crumbs from her mouth with the sleeve of a leather jacket.

She offers me a slice. I shake my head.

'I'm fine, Gran.' I sit opposite her at the table. The helmet stares straight at me. Mum calls her my mamgu as she's Welsh. Dad calls her my grandmother as he's English. I usually call her Gran so they stop arguing about it. Once I heard Dad call her a *very* bad word when he thought I wasn't listening.

'Fine is it, Cerys?' She pushes a steaming mug of tea in my direction. 'So your parents are still pretending all's quiet on the Western front in the Edwards's household, after everything?'

'I suppose…' I struggle to lift the mug to my lips with the plaster casts on.

'Tell me how you really are, my cariad.'

Silence hangs between us and mixes with the smell of cinnamon. I attempt to twirl my favourite red curl, but it was shaved off for the operation and hasn't grown back yet.

'I'm bored.' I shrug. 'I miss my friends.'

'You're talking straight now. That's more like it.' She slaps the table with her palm.

Except there's a curve to my words. I've actually missed Gran more than my friends. Visiting hours in hospital were never long enough for her stories. I give up trying to lift the mug of tea. It'll be cold soon anyway.

'You must think I'm so pathetic, Gran. Look at me—'

'Stop it right away.' She stands up and her chair shrieks against floor tiles. 'I'll hear none of that, my cariad. You're not some helpless injured bird, you're my flesh and blood.'

'But I just sit around the house doing nothing and keeping quiet and staring out of the window every day.'

She folds her arms and leans against the kitchen unit.

'Know who else does nothing and keeps quiet and stares out of windows?'

'Our neighbours' cat Tiddles?'

'Nope. A spy does all those things. Do you want to be recruited as my spy?'

I nod my head and ignore the nerves pinching away at my swollen neck.

'Good. Come with me. I've got something to show you, my cariad.'

She beckons for me to follow her through the garage's side door – I'm not usually allowed in. Too many sharp and broken things. A sickly yellow bulb flickers on and off lighting up the jumble. Here, a trampoline with a missing leg. There, a dusty plastic Christmas tree. I sneeze. Half-squeezed tubes of paint are scattered across the floor like startled rats. And an empty space in the middle. The car is being serviced again.

'It's cold,' I say, rubbing my palms together for warmth but hearing only the thin scrape of plaster cast against plaster.

'Let's be having none of that moaning, my cariad. In the war, I worked from a hut with other girls. It was freezing, dingy, and noisy as hell to boot. But it didn't matter because we were doing something. This is your hut now.'

Gran takes a torch off a shelf and rummages in a corner beside a box of magazines, their edges curled from a water leak.

'What were you like when you were young, Gran?'

'You calling me old?'

'I mean younger than you are now. During the war.'

'I was a proper stunner. Legs thin as Camel cigarettes. And I could take a corner on my motorbike faster than anyone. Never scared of nothing. That's what your tadcu – your grandad – loved best about me. Rest his soul.'

'How did you—'

'No time for an interrogation, my little spy. I found it! Have a look.'

She lifts a mint green radio onto a table spattered with oil paint. It's covered in rusty dials and a microphone is attached by a wire. There's something else I don't recognise. A device the size of Gran's hand with a flat wooden base, and a shiny brass lever on top. She presses a button on the lever to move it up and down until it emits a click. A set of battered headphones rests beside.

'This is my old amateur radio kit,' Gran says, pulling up a pair of wobbly chairs for us. 'I gave this to your grandad back when he was in hospital for chemo and feeling all lonely. Now I'm giving it to you, Cerys.'

'But I'm not in hospital anymore.'

'No. But you're lonely. Say, do you remember when Tadcu used to fall asleep in his rocking chair, and we'd cover him with as many shells and pebbles and dandelions as we could before he woke up?'

'Yeah.' I think of the time I tried to balance an apple core on his bald head when he was dozing off and laugh. My ribs ache.

Gran lowers her voice to a whisper and leans over the table towards me. 'A little bird tells me you're after a summer project, right?'

I nod.

'A proper spy needs to know Morse Code. How about I teach you?'

'Maybe. Dunno.' My wrist itches under the plaster cast.

A gentle hum hovers around the radio kit. Gran fiddles and twirls and swivels dials, before sighing and hitting it with a screwdriver. Now the static buzzes like a room of frantic bluebottles. I feel the vibrations travel up the back of my spine and my neck tingles.

'You only need to use one finger to tap out the messages on the paddle, so it don't matter if the rest of you is wrapped up like a pass-the-parcel in plaster casts.'

'I'm not sure…' I pluck at the loose thread on my jumper. It hangs like a disconnected wire.

'You might find a new friend on the air waves. You can practise Morse Code speaking to other amateur radio users.'

'But Mum and Dad say I'm not allowed to talk to strangers.'

'They won't let you talk to friends neither if they won't let you out the bloody house. I won't tell if you don't.'

Gran pulls the aerial out of the radio like she's drawing a sword. A screech escapes from the speaker and I press my casts over my ears. It reminds me of the noise I heard from the monitors when I was being rushed into surgery.

'The secret to Morse Code is treating it like a language, not a science. You have to feel the dots and dashes; turn the sound-shapes around in your mind like letters rolling on your tongue.'

She lifts a rolled-up cigarette from her jacket pocket, lights it, and takes a long drag. Each puff forms a dot of smoke and I wonder if she's signalling to me in some silent code I'm yet to learn. The glowing end is a tiny beacon in the dark.

'Okay. Yes. Can you teach me how to do it, Gran?'

'Consider it done, my cariad.'

She explains how dots and dashes stand in for letters and words. She explains the Farnsworth Method, and paddles, and listener receivers. She explains about Continuous Waves, frequencies, and Samuel Morse. It makes my head throb like it did after the accident.

We start with the basics:

Hello ....-.. .-.. — -

Yes -. — . ...

No -. — -

Bye -... -. — .

Pacing around the garage, Gran says that not long ago, on 12th July 1999, the United States' final commercial Morse Code transmission was sent. It was signed off with Samuel Morse's original 1884 message:

What hath God wrought?

(Gran spells out 'w-r-o-u-g-h-t' for me – the word feels as strange and unexpected on my tongue as it does when I tap it out in Morse.)

I realise Dad will be back from the barbecue soon. Before Gran leaves, she teaches me a final transmission:

SOS ... – -...

Gran gives me lessons a few times every week and makes me practise tapping out code in the garage until my finger throbs. She introduces me to Prosigns. N is negative, R is roger, SK is end of contact. Gran says one day I'll be able to tell from the sound-shapes whether the person on the other end of the transmission is young or old, married or single, happy or sad, honest or a liar. The truth can be found in the spaces between the symbols.

It's the middle of August and she announces I'm ready at last. Gran shows me how to use frequency to find other stations. Other people to communicate with. I turn the dial as slowly as a surgeon moves their hand during an operation. No one there. She has to leave soon, but says I must be patient when I explore the air waves. Pretend I'm a sailor in the open ocean trying to navigate my way to a spit of land. Eventually I'll find someone. She shouts 'Hwyl am nawr' and I hear the muffled revs of her bike from behind the garage door.

Today there was only silence on the radio. I try again before dinner. Nothing. I try again before bed then give up. Nights are usually quiet as the bottom of the ocean in my house, but now I hear bleeps as I drift into sleep. The hum of the fridge and the buzz of my sockets are deafening. I imagine radio waves washing over me, lulling my body into a slumber. For a moment I feel my bed sway. I reach a hand out, half expecting it to dip into cool water. Instead, the quilt is cold to my touch. In the morning I will search for land again.

Gran was right. I finally find someone on a distant frequency to practise with.

Hello. My name is Cerys.

Hello. My name is Elle.

Are you ok?

Yes.

Where do you live, Elle?

London. Where are you?

Wales. Is it sunny in London?

Yes.

Cool. How old are you, Elle?

Twelve.

Me too.

I can tell from Elle's sound-shapes she is better at Morse Code than me. There is patience in her pauses. We make plans to chat for an hour at the same time every day: twelve o'clock before our parents call us for lunch. I want to ask for longer. But I don't want my new friend to say that's enough. Stop. SK. End of contact.

When I'm doing Morse with Elle my body doesn't hurt anymore. No. That's not quite right. It still hurts, it's just that I stop noticing the pain. My body is no longer real. All I am is dots and dashes. I exist in the whirr of the radio and between clicks. We talk about music and sport and films and boys. I tell her about this guy I like in the year above me at school called Rhys. She tells me about her crush, David.

Then one muggy hot afternoon, when even the garage isn't cold anymore, Elle asks me a question I didn't expect.

Sometimes you pause for a while between messages, Cerys. Like your hand is hurting and you need rest. Are you ok?

I want to tap I-am-fine-over-and-out. For some reason I don't.

I had an accident.

Oh my God. What happened?

I should say a car hit me in the village. I went to hospital. I'm recovering. That's all. I don't. Instead, I tell Elle everything. She occasionally punctuates my frenetic taps with *sorry to hear that* or *go on*.

I tell her how the car seemed to hit me in slow motion. My feet glued to the ground. It sounds like some stupid thing from a film, but that's the truth. But the car must have been travelling fast. The cold metal launched itself into my back. Tarmac raced upwards to touch my cheek and hair. The black road turned red like a frustrated artist trying to paint over a canvas with a colour that doesn't quite cover it. The darkness still showed through.

There's a lot I don't remember. But I do remember the car that hit me. It stuck in my mind because it looked just like my mum's car. She drives a blue Volvo too. Didn't catch the number plate of the one from the crash. I remember thinking it was a weird coincidence, because hardly anyone drives through this village, let alone two navy blue Volvos in one day.

A long pause greets me at the other end of the receiver. Too long. Have I got my dots and dashes wrong?

Hello. Are you still there, Elle?

Yeah. Still here, Cerys. Go on.

Good. Do you think I am weird?

No.

I pause to rest my hand then tap again.

Maybe we can hang out sometime. Have you ever visited Wales?

Does it still hurt where the car hit you, Cerys?

Yes. All over. But I have pills for that. It is getting better.

I tell Elle that the things I'm not sure will mend are the gaps in my mind. Anything I can remember I cling to like a lifebelt. Memories are islands. Places of safety. The water in between is a blackness where the lost things go. The car's silver wheels in the sunshine are so bright they still dazzle me in my dreams.

I haven't told anyone that part about my memory before. You can fix broken bones. A broken memory is worse as there's nothing they can do about that. My parents worry a lot. The worst thing is I can't remember if my friends haven't been to visit yet because I never had any, or if I had friends and they forgot about me while I was in hospital.

Elle. Will you remember to message me at the same time tomorrow?

Course I will, silly.

I have to go. Dad is calling me. Speak then Bye.

Except Elle isn't on the other end of the radio the next day. Or the day after. The frequency goes dead. I must have messed up. It was meant to be a fun chat with a friend to practise Morse Code. But I mentioned my accident. Elle freaked out. It wasn't fun anymore.

The symbols for SOS play over and over and over in my mind until my head aches.

... − -...

I want it to stop, so I push the radio off the table. Gran's radio. It shatters into a hundred little pieces. This garage is a place for sharp and broken things only. I didn't cry after the accident. Doctors and nurses and family thought it was strange. But I'm crying now. Not even Mamgu, orange squash and chocolate biscuits will make this better.

In the silent dark I shout hello. Nothing echoes back.

Three quick taps at my bedroom door. Dad's special knock. My parents knew I was feeling "off" yesterday, but I didn't tell them about Elle or the broken radio.

'Hi, sweetheart. Look at that blue sky through your curtains! Aren't we lucky with the weather this week?'

I nod. 'Yes, Dad.'

'Your mum and I wanted to have a word with you about something. Would you come and join us in the kitchen? I'll help you down. We're baking bread for breakfast.'

That little vein in Dad's forehead pulses when he's stressed. It's pulsing now. Mum is pacing past the kitchen units like Gran does. She's still wearing her paint-spattered apron. There's an emerald splash on the front of it. Green. Maybe today will be a good day? Her eyes look pink and tired. They are unable to meet mine.

'Best you sit down, my cariad,' Mum says. 'What we're about to say might come as a bit of a shock.'

The kitchen smells of fresh dough but my appetite has gone. Dad pulls a chair out and helps lower me into it.

'We wanted to tell you sooner, but we were trying to avoid anything overstimulating or distressing in your current state,' he says, nodding at Mum.

'What do you mean?'

Mum smooths down her apron with fingers bitten to the quick. A starling's beak taps against the birdfeeder by the window.

'Your gran – Mamgu – passed away recently. It was peaceful in her sleep. Heart gave out. No pain. We've been trying to decide the best way to break the news, my cariad.'

I sit there and say nothing and blink. Mum and Dad stare back at me, then at each other, as if I am communicating in some alien code they cannot decipher. Strips of sunlight force their way through slats in the blind.

I take my water pistol from its hiding place under the sink, fill it up, and head outside into the garden to play.

Close in Time, Space or Order

Meredith Miller

The bus swung out along a drop, around a curve and down into a little green depression full of sheep. It didn't take very many sheep to fill the dip, or long to pass through it and up onto the next rise, the next bit of rock too hard to be eaten by the sea. Or eaten very soon, anyway. In the layer of time in which Linette sat on the bus, it was a thing that would never happen. Most rocks were permanent for her.

She sat against the inside window, adding her body to the balance against empty air. A woman watched her from further up the bus, as if maybe Linette were familiar, but she wasn't sure.

'Linnie?'

She looked like anyone's mother. Anyone whose mother rode the bus.

Linette didn't flinch or turn. She kept her eyes black and still, as though she'd borrowed them from one of the sheep. Anyone's Mother stood up and moved three seats toward her, holding on to the headrests while the bus swung round the high bend.

'Linnie Ross? It is, isn't it? My God!'

Linette looked out the window like she didn't quite know how to use the borrowed eyes, pretending she hadn't heard that infant version of her own name. If you'd been near enough, you'd have seen the little tremor run through her.

'I guess I've changed,' the woman said.

Linette turned then. 'I'm sorry — '

'I've not seen you in years. You've lived abroad, haven't you? It's me, Ellen.'

'I think you — '

'From the shop?'

'I'm not.' It wasn't an unfinished sentence. You'd have seen the full stop hit home with Ellen from the shop.

'I'm so sorry, I thought — God, how strange, you look just like a friend of mine. I'm so sorry.'

Anyone's Mother — Ellen — moved back up the bus, and for the first time Linette felt glad she was home. It would never have worked in Spain or Greece, that.

The bus stop came before the village was visible. The shelter might have been anywhere, nowhere, unless you already knew what was round the curve behind the tall grass.

Linette stepped out into the lay by while the front suspension was still hissing. Ellen watched from the bus, maybe hurt or angry or suspicious, but there was a layer of glass between them now, an engine and a timetable. It didn't matter that Linette had given herself away. She'd be gone again before Ellen talked enough to get the visitors coming. People would hesitate, wouldn't they?

Linette walked along the narrow shoulder, past a pair of women's pants hanging from the long grass, rotting in the salt. At the further arm of the bend, the grass faded and the world opened out along a strand, a spill of houses and a pile of cement blocks dumped in front of the worst poundings of the winter sea. A wide mouth in the side of the country, or something bitten out.

She turned to the beach. Empty. No dog walkers, no

weekenders, no cockle pickers or honeymooners. Certainly not her, in a summer dress and bare feet, sitting on something that wasn't there either. Not her, in army-green trousers tied around her little waist with a string. Her, holding a gritty hand out and down for Linette to grab onto. Standing fast, sinking in the sand while the waves pulled at Linette's knees.

Instead, there were four empty parking spaces and one dirty van lined up facing the beach.

A man stood with his toes to the sea wall and his hand held open to the sky, gloved and full of some kind of rubbish that was attractive to gulls. A screaming blur of wings all around him until he caught sight of Linette at the edge of it. He tossed whatever it was onto the sand and turned, peered forward then straightened his spine. He knew her but she didn't know him.

Keep walking. Look away.

'Alright, Linnie?'

She did, of course. Know him. He was old now. Of course.

'Graham.'

Together they looked away toward the water and the sharp empty flat of the sand. He could see her on the beach, too. Not see her.

'I didn't— It's lovely to see you, Graham.'

He kept his body and his eyes facing outward. 'I could have fetched you from the train, cariad.'

'I didn't want to be a bother.'

'Where are your things?'

'It's just— ' Linette half turned so he could see her rucksack.

'No one's been in the house for ages, you know. Where will you sleep?'

'I don't think I'll— I have my sleeping bag. Don't worry. Please.'

'Not staying, then.'

'I am. I've come for some of her things. An archive in London— '

Graham let out a huff of air from the back of his throat. He had lines now, spoked around his eyes. Eyes like chips of glass pushed into the skin.

'I am back, though. In the UK, I mean. But the house— '

'Are there groceries with you? Come and get in.' Graham waved the empty gull hand over his shoulder at the van. 'I'll run you up.'

'No need.'

'It's no trouble. Come on.'

'I want to walk. A bit of time, Graham.'

Four words too many, escaped from the pile filling up her lungs and slipped out from between her teeth. Now Graham would have to carry them. She hadn't even passed the empty fish and chips kiosk, not even up onto the road and already she'd spat her regurgitated bones at the first person along the beach, frightened the wings from Graham's hand and replaced them with words unwanted.

The words weren't gone from her either, but his now and all. That is how a curse works.

'Well, I'm along the way if you do want something.' He flung out the hand again, throwing nothing over the sea wall, and got into the van.

Linette went up the old road, climbing the open side of the hill. From a distance it might have been anything she was carrying on her back. Rucksack or child. Laundry bag or a sack full of empty light. Impossible to guess the weight from the way she walked beneath it.

There was no sun in the world now. The blanket of grey over the sea was working hard to hide them all, the waves trying to erase that string of houses from the edge of the country. In three hundred years there would be boat trips on clear days. People under a pitiless sky would look down at them, half buried in sand under sterile currents full of heavy metals and invisible particulate.

'Did I think she would be real, really there?' She spoke out loud on the empty road, which might have been the second sign of madness, after half believing the dream of her mother on the beach.

'She wasn't there.'

That is, not where Linette had expected her to be. Not where she always was in the place in Linette's head that was this place. Inside there, she'd been on the beach beyond the car park, in a dress people would call coral, but it wasn't. Coral is basically bone, isn't it? This was some kind of orange-pink like the 1960s, some very girlish colour that would have been vintage even when Linette was small. Inside Linette's head, and before she had arrived, her mother was perched on a convenient rock which wasn't there either. A big rock half buried in the sand like in films of California. The colour of her hair came from one of those films too. Not just in Linette's head, it actually did.

Does. Had.

Linette looked down from the road, through the present muffled light. She had brought her actual body to the actual place, and the beach was empty here. Absent of rocks for seating and of her. Graham had driven off and now there were only the white lines and the two streetlamps at the edge of the car park below, dwarfed by January waves. Nothing else or more.

At the house the front door swung open easily, not a bit swollen. The paper still lay smooth over the walls in the vestibule, but the smell of the carpets was thick enough to have its own colour and sound. Right away it filled her ears and coated the lining of her throat. She swam through it, opening windows.

There was electric and water. No one ever turns them off, no matter how long the meters go without ticking over. Linette made a circuit of the rooms, pulling cords and turning taps, trying to read the stains on things. Most of the bulbs were worn out and she lost track of the number of her pulls, of whether light should be shining or not.

Everything would of course be damp; she'd brought a dry section of someone's *Telegraph* from the train, and a tin of matches that was part of her everyday life anyway. In the kitchen she found a pair of wooden salad spoons. Maybe enough to start on but they'd smoke for ages. She put them in the sitting room grate, lit some paper under them and carried on upstairs. There were no shelves left, no desk, no piles of printing, no portable tannoy or climbing belts. Boxes in the loft, maybe?

On the landing, the paper was peeling like burned skin. She stripped it off and piled it at the top of the stairs. The rope dangling from the loft hatch felt greasy and the light pull did nothing to dispel the dark above. In the morning, then.

She went back down the stairs with her arms full of wallpaper and a fine dust of mould settling onto her clothes, working its way into her nostrils and her lungs. The living room fire was drawing the smoke, but the spoons were barely charred. More paper, more smoke, and out flew a red admiral. Turning to follow it, she saw another on the ceiling. The kind her nan called a chimney sweep, maybe. Not enough light to tell, now. She'd woken them from their winter sleep in the chimney, and it felt worse than anything she'd done here. In the end the confused butterflies on the ceiling were the thing that choked her and made thick, dirty water rise up in her eyes.

In the kitchen the gas had run out, but Linette had brought a camping stove and a canister. She unfolded bedding and tea bags, a towel and a pot, a string of lights with batteries attached, things she always carried with her from farm to farm under the actual sun in other countries where she was contained, sufficient. Where she stepped like a ghost and no one felt her passing. If not for Graham, she might have done the same here. Slipped in and slipped out without anyone hearing the noise inside her.

Gagging, she dragged a pile of bedroom carpet down the stairs to the sitting room, dumped it onto some brown stains and then went up to make her bed on the bare boards. Keeping to the use of each room, she lit her stove and made soup in the kitchen. The stains had not stopped her, the carpet smell, the pattern still visible through the greasy dust on the curtains.

But then there was the back door, leading from the kitchen to the porch. The splintered frame. She fell back against the worktop and stared at it while the dark came down one layer at a time and silted up around her.

Until the only light in the kitchen came from the gas she had not turned off, the little burner casting blue onto the worktop. She could no longer see the broken lock with the flat dark eyes of her body. Inside her head, spikes of broken wood around it showed yellow and smelled of sap. She lit a match and carried it over behind a cupped hand. The wood was grey, of course, exposed to thick air and carpet mould for so many seasons. When she touched it with the match it took a full minute to blacken. Still it wouldn't catch, though it smoked a mushroom-smelling smoke.

The wings beat first against a corner of the ceiling behind

her, and then on the back of her neck. She dropped the match and reached back. The thing fluttered past her ear, slow and drowsy with January, like anyone woken in the middle of an arc of sleep.

There were three more in the bedroom, come down from the open loft and beating like little spring winds against the ceiling. One landed pale green beneath her book light. It made small shadows, interrupting her sentences, then enormous wings thrown against the far walls. Anyway, she was too tired to read. No, not tired. Sleepy.

She was there underneath Linette's sleep of course, like some kind of angel without a comprehensible size, wearing that coral dress that might never have existed, but was there now lying translucent over the beach like a final layer at the bottom of the sky.

Standing beneath her, Linette felt the wings against her neck. She reached a hand up and touched something soft and cold on the back of her own head. She could see it, a flap of skin the colour of dead people, a slice of meat beneath it and then a curved window of bone the size of a fifty-pence piece.

'Wait. This isn't— '

'You'll have to do the carpets, Sweetpea.'

'—my head. Why are you making me— '

'You'll have to do the carpets, then you can go out.'

'I don't need to see this.'

'He walked away, Linnie. Remember? He walked away. You've done nothing wrong.' Her mother's hair was the purple-silver of the inside of shells people bring back from holiday.

The shells they used for ashtrays thirty years ago when Linette was small and the house was full of people and little pills and smoke. When stockings hung from the shower curtain rail because women wore them and then washed them out in the sink. When other women left impressions on the beds where they sat, fresh from their first bath in weeks, telling about what it was like to live chained to a tree, while someone cooked downstairs and her mother sat against the headboard singing, soft. When the rim of the bathtub was covered in candle wax and someone cried for her underneath the windows all summer long.

In the dream, she in the coral dress was the woman from then. Her face was the face from a memory of climbing the hill out back, one day in the wind. From the time when Linette saw her only from below.

Linette still had her fingers in the wound.

'This isn't my head!'

'Open the windows.'

'It obviously isn't mine. I can see the back of it.'

Lightning flashed between them, pinning the sky to the surface of the sea.

'Air out the cabinets, and then you can go.'

It flashed again and Linette covered her eyes with dripping hands. The liquid on her fingers wasn't blood. It was something else that comes from inside people's heads, something yellow and viscous and essential. And then her mother fell out of the sky and they were on the sand, both inside everyday bodies, and the lightning flashed a third time.

Linette opened her eyes in the dark, what should have been the dark. For a moment it was full of sharp blue light. Then darkness, then the light again. She closed her eyes and opened them a second time, but the lightning from inside her was still flashing in the room. It took some time to understand that she had pulled the light string one too many times. The bulb was whole but the wiring was frayed, wet. It had taken however many hours for seeping water to carry the current across the gap.

She might have burned in her bed, been anaesthetised by the smoke and never woken, slipped out of the world still looking up at the lightning from the beach inside her. She pulled the cord and fell back down into uninterrupted dark.

In the morning, the loft was full of more wood too damp to burn, and very little light. There was a box though, packed with flyers from the M3 protest and some newsletters made at Greenham. And there were dozens more butterflies, folded and sleeping with their legs stuck to the roof joists. Painted ladies and meadow browns drinking in the mould through the powder on their wings.

The box was promising, but it wasn't enough.

Linette's friend Dan worked for a place called the Something History Workshop now. They had an archive and, he said, an acquisitions fund. It could be enough to set her up in a flat, enough for a hostel while she waited on the housing list. Dan said the borough council might put her anywhere these days. Apply in London and you'd wind up in Gateshead or Plymouth. Well, fine. Linette was happy for them to close their eyes and place her with a pin in a map.

The archive wanted flyers and things from the road protests, from Greenham and the CND. They might take letters and diaries, if they had 'significance' which, apparently, a thing could objectively have.

They did not want to hear about all the kinds of women who'd been jumbled up together in the house, about what that was like. The slow bloody violence of bodies breaking free. They didn't even know to ask about that, because it was the thing that was actually lost.

She finished burning the salad spoons and then fed the upstairs wallpaper to the fire piece by piece. Where else could she look? There was no basement. The slate floors sat right on the bare earth, which was the reason for the damp. Her mother would never have those floors pulled up. Linette found a signed copy of *Woman and Nature* and some drafts of something in the cabinet built into the side of the fire.

In the kitchen, one of the cupboards was stuck. Things had settled and two doors in the corner were in the way of each other, wedged shut. There were no tools in the house, no kitchen utensils bigger than her own fork even, now that she'd burned the salad spoons. She could look in the garden for a stone to bash the cabinet door.

That was the mistaken thought, the one that threw her back. The house had fooled her into imagining something harder than bone. She'd never have gone physically through that door, past that splintered frame onto the grass. But her body wasn't necessary.

He had grown tired of crying for her in the back garden, and then of shouting outside until he'd woken the whole house. After he'd banged so hard with bare fists that the doorframe splintered, he came through it with blood and hanging skin on his knuckles, shouting that he wanted his things. People had stumbled up from the sitting room; they were crowded round the kitchen door, sleepy-eyed and swearing.

Linette's mother had shrunk against that corner cabinet, breathing so that you could see the heart pounding inside her, mouth open and showing her pink tongue. You'd swear she was physically smaller than she had been minutes before. Other times, she could fill a crowded room until everyone in it felt they were next to her. She was like that, full of glamours and tricks.

She, Linette, had grown a clear six inches that summer, so that she looked down at her mother's shoulders, folded forward over the heart. He was still shouting, and it wasn't hard for Linette to reach him now with the whetstone. She didn't know it was the whetstone. It was closed into her hand without her having thought about picking it up. If you are frightened enough, if you are not yet used to your height or your strength, if you are defending your shrunken animal mother crouched in the corner, thinking doesn't come into it.

He walked away out that door again. He is still walking now, though he can't speak without lisping. To hear him, you'd think he had a difficult birth, without enough blood or oxygen to his brain. Linette heard his pressed, breathy voice many times after, his crippled shouts in the road, at the police station, in the chippy when she went in with her college friends.

He had walked out the door again without staggering even, so that Linette saw the back of his head looking whole. The blood, the sticky flap of skin, the circle of bone, were hidden beneath his dirty hair.

Over the following weeks women began to drift off. Linette had swung the sharpening stone and cleared them all away. By spring, the two of them were alone in the house like any mother and daughter, sharing packets of Amber Leaf and a housing allowance. When October came round again, she went away. It was six months more before Linette shook the dazed light from her eyes and left the country.

In the end she kicked the corner cabinet in. Nothing in there but more sleeping butterflies, clinging to the chipboard under the worktop, too drowsy to startle and flutter out. The cabinet doors burning in the fire smelled like weed killer. Their smoke made Linette short of breath and two more butterflies dropped from a corner of the ceiling to the floor.

Graham was on the beach still. Again. There was a child with him, wearing frog wellies and a bicycle helmet. God, a grandchild. It must be. Graham was holding a stick, drawing a picture for the little girl in the wet sand. Linette walked toward them without shrinking or turning her eyes.

'Alright?' He didn't look up from his picture, which was a face like the one that had fallen out of the sky the night before.

'Where is she, Graham?'

He frowned over at the grandchild whom he hadn't introduced.

'I'm sorry, I— Hello. I'm Linette.'

'This is Rose Ellen. Are you going to say hello, Rose E?'

She didn't. He had stopped drawing. The child had already begun to lose interest before the words made her shy and she turned toward the water, pretending not to hear. She was maybe five, born years after the house had emptied.

'I see her so often you'd think she was dead.' Linette's voice, flat as the sand.

He looked up then. She saw herself through him, rounder now, with crow's feet, nervous fingers always moving like she was threading invisible lace. Her hair was no colour at all. To him she must look like time itself.

'They didn't press charges against you for a reason, bach.'

'Yes, but the reason wasn't because I was innocent. She messed with him. She didn't really mean to, but people went mad around her.'

They turned toward the water together, looking out at something bobbing beyond the breakers, an eye above the surface or a knot of wood.

'He was twenty-three years old,' she said. 'So young.'

'You were fifteen.'

'Sixteen.'

Linette breathed in the salty light, the amniotic scent of kelp, the death of a skate, specifically a skate, that she could smell but not see.

'When I saw her first wrinkles, I thought the people would stop coming because women with wrinkles don't matter any more. I was so relieved to see her getting old.'

'She was younger than you are now.'

'Now I know that doesn't happen. You don't matter, but they keep right on coming anyway.'

The child, Rose Ellen, walked the tide line, but she wasn't looking for treasure. She looked dead ahead and carefully placed her feet one in front of the other like she was on a circus wire.

'I shoved the stone in my pocket and ran down here,' Linette said. 'I walked up and down the beach for hours. I was so dizzy I thought I'd pass out and fall down, that the tide would come in and cover me before I came to. I hoped for that, I guess.'

'Stay, Linnie. Fix up the house. Why pay to live somewhere else when the place is there? Make it new.'

He only said that because he needed her there. They always need you in places like this. They want to watch you rise and fall.

'I guess she would have been different if she could have.'

Linette let Graham take her back to the station in the van. How could she not?

She climbed into the passenger seat and put the box of things she hoped were historically significant down on the mat by her feet.

There was no need to turn her head to see the houses and the sea defence disappear from the rear window. She looked instead at the rotting pair of pants still waving from the long grass near the lay-by, at a figure in the bus shelter with a bobble hat and a wheelie cart, someone else half familiar who had become old in the interval. Graham felt warm and used on the seat beside her, like maybe fathers feel when you are past having your own children, when you have circled a minor ocean and come back to them. There was only a thin humming space between them in the cab, full of the smell of mud and old milk.

Foolscap

Anthony Shapland

Like a beacon, the summit catches the early sun.

B stares up at it, waiting in the dim light of the kitchen. Drowsy and nervous. Coffee scalds the hob with a hiss and he rouses himself. An excitement flushes through his body, like a soundwave.

He packs and unpacks a bag in anticipation. Leftover food from the leftover, uncounted days at the year's end. Gold-wrapped chocolates spill across the counter. Toffees that cloy on gums and pull fillings and are best avoided.

This house is council new. New-ish. New enough to feel displaced, temporary. A single cul-de-sac of interlocking brick driveways smother the earth below. Rainwater run-off rills from concrete edges in icy sheets. All on one level. Accessible. Grab-handy handles and wipeable surfaces and the smell of Dad's ashtrays and mince, which lingers, even after all these months.

A fitted kitchen, fitted bedrooms, fitted carpets and ill-fitted doors, which close with soft cushions of air. Frustrated doorslams dissipate in damp corridors. Weightless cardboard interiors and hollow aluminium handles spring click. A plasterboard-thin unit of rooms clinging to an indifferent hill.

In the bath, he scrubs himself all over, again and again. Carbolic froth ebbs and ripples. A leg hangs to cool as he lifts his hips to wash below. Liquid rises in his ears as he sinks, his body a pink island in the milky, clouded water.

The coming expedition feels parallel, separate, unreal. It hangs just below the surface of his mind, a confusion of fear and shame and excitement. He's not quite sure what he's walking towards. A pulling and a pushing; his instinct to go, his anxiety to stay. Either choice feels wrong. He can't not act. He can't stop the buzz, the vibration. The hunger.

They had talked at the bar. The shopkeeper was buying a round for loyal customers. A large round. All smiles and Christmas. Hands and spills and drinks passed over shoulders in odd-shaped glasses, and tonic and snacks and nuts gripped in clenched jaws and have you got a straw? Four straws, ice and a slice, and two more pints and one for the barman and good cheer and broad laughter. Sorry. Are you waiting? Here, let me get yours. And he did.

With drinks delivered, the shopkeeper stood apart, unnoticed. Beer froth on a dark beard, a mid-distance stare. Then a shift, a slight difference in his posture. Or a change in his face. Maybe just a pause. He looked sad. No, not sad, just alone. B recognised something he couldn't name.

It doesn't make sense to him now, but just like that, he turned to the shopkeeper and cheers-ed him. He never does that.

At the edge of different regulars' territory, staked in coats and handbags, they stood, together. He knew him before that meeting at the club. Good natured, M, the shopkeeper, the hardware shop in the village, handy, knows his stock, knows his decorating kit. He'd never looked at him properly before. Small talk. Christmas. Doing anything? Family? Quiet one. Same.

He bought him a drink back. Christmas after all.

Night's end, tinsel gaudy and rasping, a festive singalong, then one for the road. He was drunk. They were both drunk. M pulled a sheet of foolscap from a pad above the payphone. A time and date, about a week from then, written twice then torn; half each. An agreement. Every year, before the next, he heads to the stone at the highest point. It's the one time the shop shuts. There's a view.

The music ended, suddenly. Everyone cheered. Eyes flinched from an abrupt strip-light glare, shiny faces in an electric spark and flutter. Pints gulped. Coats, party-hats, bodies steamed in the cold air.

When he woke the next day, the yellow, lined paper was still in his pocket. He couldn't quite remember what it meant, fogged and dry-mouthed. Slurred handwriting, a torn edge: *31st noon, '87*. His half of their agreement. Gradually, B recalls the smiling face that fleetingly looked like his own.

He clears an arc in the mirror steam. He dislikes shaving, dabs some abandoned *Brut 33* over his stubbly chin. Too much, overpowering, he coughs. He scrubs it off, his cheeks pink and shining.

Held in the palm of the valley below, a freezing fog flows with the river. Winter pale, above, the slope is gridded with larch. At least the climb will be warm, he tells himself, pulls a red peaked cap low over his eyes and hunches against the cold.

He calls a goodbye to no-one but habit.

The lowland has been left to sour, compacted, newbuild clay. Water slicks its brownfield surface in frost above the river and road, the railway and town. The air is chill and he shudders. The valley is shrinking. Houses fall apart, worthless. A place of industry sagging, starved of purpose, underfed. Graffitied *Scab* in a made-clean scrubbed stone scar. Drainage ditches choke with briars that scratch into the pasture. Flag iris fan where reeds clump. Marginals thrive in the lost farm's soggy decline and grass cedes to scrub, white with hoar.

On the shallow incline, bog-soft and glazed with ice, the ground cracks, sucks and pulls. His legs swing an awkward pendulum, mud-heavy boots clod.

The hill rises above the town, tipped from mining spoil, load by load. An unnatural mound poured from above, like sand funnelled in a slow hourglass. It grew until it settled, leaning back on the hollow east mountain behind. Unstable, weighty twins. Land held with trees in fear of slip.

B peers into the forest. Resolve drops from his mind momentarily. Everything feels motionless, prop-like. Scenery thrown up in haste. The man-made plantation gridding a man-made mountain.

A Jay swoops low, bounces, and takes alarm up to the canopy. Lines of trees open and close with a pulse of shadow as he walks. Light filters onto deep soft-dropped layers of needles that make for a quieter tread. Roots bind tree to tree, holding the slope and rocking the dense floor as a breeze takes high branches in pulls and sways. He is aware of the bird's silent side-eye high above, the sweep of branches that whisper in scrapes and feathers of air.

He closes his eyes, lets other senses navigate.

This hill is a bright map of his childhood. A play track for stunt bikes, a den, a place to get lost in, to disappear in, alongside siblings. Or away from them. A place to loiter and mischief dull school days out until the bell. A place to be alone. Alone with this feeling that he's not the same as his brothers. Knowing instinctively that some part of himself is best off hidden

How often he has stared into the mirror at this hidden him. An understudy, carefully learning lines, behaviours; in the wings waiting to take the stage. Trying to understand how it is to be in this small town, a boy in this world.

He sings quietly to this other self walking alongside him. Any song he knows. Lyrics escape his memory and whistling fills the gaps when words don't come. Unembarrassed, his choir-learnt bassy-baritone sounds out, clear but sad, without a soprano lift. He tries falsetto until the sound makes him smile, then notes flatten into melancholy.

With eyes closed he isn't alone, his own footsteps come back to him. He pauses; the other him pauses. He moves through the vertical planes of trees with himself in parallel, neither hunter or hunted. Obscured, hidden between columns of warm bark.

His pace is steady. Ahead, toward the clearing, he can see the tips of larch, amber and fiery. With the rise, the ray of sun that reaches further into the valley will meet him, or he will climb to meet it.

His song stops. Sounds that bowed soft vibrations in foliage play staccato and sharp. Abruptly the line of trees ends. He blinks a brighter light and stands on the edge of desolation. No longer the warm, acidic, compress of forest carpet. Cleared trunks and scrub and a dry smell. A diesel smell. The forest cull. Breakers stripped and replanted methodically.

The wreckage is silver, bony and torn. Ruts change the path to a difficult clamber. Branches and trees, clipped and stacked by machinery, are unkind. Here is the tipping point of the mine-spoil, the spout where the ground turns inside-out, the moving mountain, black and shimmering and unstable.

Stumbling, he is suddenly tired. He rests.

The days that led him here were eased by a hangover and nervy excitement. It felt far off, distant, possible. Now he is ambushed by hesitancy, a judder of confusion. He wonders if he's being a fool.

He sinks back into the grass. It's cold and damp and he lies low, out of sight. A buzzard circles overhead. He imagines it slowing mid-air, wings back, before plummeting toward him, snatching his pathetic body up from the grass.

What the hell is he thinking?

Suddenly he is nervous. He knows only too well what he's doing out here on this bare hill. He wants to pay attention to the bearded man, with curled hairs at his collar, who smiled. He wants to feel all those things he shouldn't feel, think or seek.

He gets up, his throat tenses in a grip that augers tears, or nausea, or grief. He understands the stir in his gut; why he washed so attentively; why he's wearing his good clothes, new clothes with labels that scratch. He'll go to hell for what he wants, but still he climbs.

And there he is. The shopkeeper, M, in the distance.

The ground is softer. The spring of grass and moss and rock is kinder, the air clear. Sheep tracks ring the slope like ribbons and wool tufts on gorse with pink and blue smit marks. Ferns curl bright fiddleheads through grey earth. The breeze is keen. He feels his shoulders ease, his lungs open. The day is short, just past the shortest, but the clear sky makes it feel endless.

M squints into the bright sun as they cross the plateau. Cold-bitten pink cheeks; he waves a gloved hand. They both pause. Nerves slow into stillness. They walk toward each other and to the platform of rock at the highest point.

Men with men, mates. B knows how to be with his brothers, with friends, how he used to be with his dad. Hesitant steps. How to behave, how far apart to sit, what to talk of.

Suddenly they are strangers together, as on a train, limbs and bodies settle, close but distinct.

The buzzard's silent circling soothes as their eyes follow the spiral and fall of its search. Glancing sideways, the shopkeeper's face is near. A drip shivers under his nose at the top of a dark beard. His green eyes shine with tears.

Two breaths meet in a single drifting vapour and they sit and look out over the hills.

They both remember they've brought food. A winter picnic of sorts. The crackle of foil, a sandwich teased in two. Squashed mince pies and a shared thermos of coffee, which splatters away from their lips in the breeze.

The conversation eases with the sharing. The land ahead maps out their stories of relatives and memories and school. More gestures than chat, they say little. The sway of the story and the rhythm of sounds settle between them. They talk in roundabout ways, circling a centre like the buzzard's spiral and fall.

They find common ground. Step forward and back in words and codes and invitations and pauses. They run out of the things they can say easily, but the silence is comfortable. Side by side, they face south and talk to the hills.

The sun is overhead. Ears blush cold, sparks light hazel eyes.
A crumb of pastry is lost in his dark beard.
Their shadows get shorter,
two parallel lines.

Equal.

Mirrored.
A lone cloud idles.
They gaze straight ahead,
suspended from life, excused from time.

M takes a toffee, cold, hard and sweet. He ends each year on this hill, quiet. This year as he climbed, vaguely and without directing things, he felt he might understand more from up here. He hoped he'll be understood, that he'll be more than *the man from the shop*.

He rolls a yellow cellophane square. Unrolls it. Jaws a sweet-chewed figure of eight. Speech is stuck on the horizon. The sun drifts west and a breeze lifts.

M feels the weight of the two bottles of stout in his bag, a gift from a shop customer. He forgot an opener, sorry, but offers them; B deftly upturns one bottle over the other. A satisfying twist, *psh*. Caps lift.

They clink, a cold swig sinks warm, tart after sweet.

Chat, unstopped, pours in drink. They talk about building things, farms, pit closures and hasty, propped-up factories. Their ambitions. Blushing red as his cap, B confesses that he wants to be a painter, to properly learn. Muddy feet swing free. Proper like. Decorating's a step in the right direction, he reckons.

They lean, in gossip about the village, about the shop and work. Under the peak of his cap, his brow lowers, the strike. The anger, the divisions. His brothers picketing. They raise a solemn *cheers* in respect of the newly formed dead dad club.

B talks about wanting to leave, to see more. He feels trapped without a real job, without a trade. The river, the road and the railway go just one direction. It feels small. Everybody belongs to someone else. Nothing changes. A sigh in clouded breath.

Fingers shred the bottle label. He talks slowly. The cap hides his face. His throat is taut, his voice catches. He plucks blades of grass. A careful balance. He steps forward on each word.

He needs to change something. He doesn't feel like he belongs, he loves his brothers and sisters, but feels like he'll never fit. His jaw-tight clench pulses where his cap sits. Their arms brush. B turns. His moist breath warmer and closer than the cool air.

Beneath the words, trust is signalled. Shared and private. An agreement. A foolscap date. No lies.

M seeks words to offer in response, but the right ones don't come. He tries to nudge a sentence into life. Some meaningful sign of understanding. He wants, more than anything, to talk for longer but, as soon as the thought arrives, he's like an actor left without a script.

He looks inward to something he can't speak aloud. Something he rolls toward in countless night grunts. An imagined climax, forbidden, hidden in shame behind locked toilet doors, under heavy blankets that pin down the sin, the wretched. The hunger for another body, for a person to know, to see what he knows. To share.

He feels caught out, seen doing something he ought not. Sadness sinks through him in an obscure confusion of fear and shame. The heavy impossibility of the shop, of the valley below.

He's filled with guilt. What is he doing up here?

He blurts out that he should get home to his daughter.

A mouth opens to reply. Then swallows the sentence.

Why did he say that? His daughter lives with her mother and her stepdad, real dad, a better dad than the grieving boy-dad he cut, trying to fix something in him. An alibi. He feels disgusted at his life. A shopkeeper, sad and alone. A cold claws through the stone in shivers.

I don't have a daughter; I mean I do have a daughter. She's great. But she's not at home. It's just me. Just me for years since Tigger died. The cat. Sorry. He falters.

Soon they both sit and stare at the ground as if some important memory is lost.

A long wait.
They peer down into the valley.

B lifts his red cap and nudges the shopkeeper.
Daughter – you dark horse, you!

Ease returns like a clear note in a song. A glance and, in their
shared deep broad smile, shame lifts. A longer look, a stare,
unashamed. Its end acknowledged in a nod. Settled.

A hand on his shoulder, their goodbye. Sincere. The new thread
connecting them thrums as they start to move. Long-sat legs
move slowly. M feels big and clumsy, shy. An animal learning
to be wild again after long performing tricks.

They walk without turning away. B waves, his red cap raised,
sunlight on an open face, a smile. He sinks below the east
horizon. He shouts, hands cupped, mute, until the word glides
into the listener's ear, *thanks*.

Happy new year the shopkeeper calls as he starts his own walk
west.

M steadies himself for the first steps over the edge. This stretch
is steep. Muddy footholds worn in sod, pockets in roots and
rocks and wiry grass. On heels, leaning back, legs move ahead
of his body, knees jar in a sharp descent.

With a gasp he grabs a tree and holds tight and hugs tight, an
anchor. A beery belch through a smile, his tongue tastes sweet
crumbs in his beard. He feels drunker than he should and
giggles. He tips forward in baby steps. The slope rolls to a trot,
a run, faster, skimming stones and air as feet land heavy. He is
above the ground, wild and laughing.

He wants to leap high and yell out all the things he didn't say. How he hasn't felt like this before, that he doesn't know what it is, but it isn't wrong; then gravity tips and turns and the hill shrugs him, light as air, toward home.

A slide, his bum bounces until a pile of leaves slows him to a stop. M laughs in surprise and his head rests with beetles and worms. In his mind an image of B lingers, arriving with the sun behind him, hair caught like fire. A halo, a red glow of light through cold ears, a shy wave.

thanks, on a breeze.

The shopkeeper looks up at bare branches bathed in sun, breathes clouds of bright amber as his chest rises and falls. Lichen furs oak and birch. Evening light glows. The silent bed-warm rot of winter is soft. Roots fix deep in the soil, reaching through streams and fissures to hold on to the unmined rock below. Whatever happens next, it is a good thing.

A sphere uncurls. A woodlouse navigates this new obstacle to sink from his shoulder into leaves.

M sits up. He knows this place. They foraged here, before everything changed; it fed his dad's fondness for anything free, his mam's despair at the grocer's wilting offerings. He wonders at her, mushrooms in her skirt apron, slim dirty fingers in earth. As he walks he remembers; bolete, chantarelle, inkcaps. He tastes crab-apple bullets made sweet; the sherbet flowers, berries of the Elder, *the Judas tree*; papery hazelnuts in the paws of thieving squirrels, wimberries stuffed in pint bottles, stained mouths with sticky, smiling teeth.

His father held him close. The part of her he could keep safe, after she died. In her place he worked hard, laughed hard, learnt the trade. He was all the sons and daughters that never came. The shopkeeper *& Son* became self-sufficient, just the two of them. M filled the gaps and siphoned play into work. His options narrowed. His path was set. Then his dad slowly faded. Like a light going out.

And now it's just him. The shop fills his waking hours, his dreams. It is the soundtrack of every day. It is his familiar, M, the *& Son*.

The trail is hard to follow in the low sun that flashes on motes of dust and shines on every dropping leaf. Lekking gnats weave sparks. The glare floats on his retina, even if he shields his eyes. He strays. He reorients. His interrupted rhythm is wrong.

The afternoon shadow rises and as he sinks below the air clears, cold. A brittle crunch of frost in the leaves and glassy puddles' icy contours. Meltwater trickles a bubbling echo into the drainage pipe funnelling it beneath the village.

He acts his part in that small world. The village. A community, where the same money just gets passed around without ever seeming to multiply. The shop keeps it moving and he is the shopkeeper's boy-shopkeeper. His father's mantra: solve problems; answer questions; clean up messes; take pride; be useful; needed. Liked.

In the shop, he is their mirror; he's one of them. On the side of the useless never-get-round-to-it husband; in sympathy with practical wives; lazy sons should take it easier; enthusiastic brothers, go-for-it. He coos over babies with doting grandparents, and arms pragmatic daughters with the right tools. He offers credit to the disinherited, those who never clear a tab. He is diplomatically on all sides in feuds or squabbles. All their lives held in a matrix of problem gutters, stained carpets and woodworm.

It adds to all he carries. M holds it all, a complex ledger of lives written over half a century and more, a history of the village through a family shop. The keeper.

And what do they know of him? Who holds his story, his truth? If he dies tomorrow, they will all fade a little. All those reflections he offers back to them, day after day. He will fall, silent, confiding in nobody.

Sometimes he feels cheated. Taken for a fool. There are things he knows he will never have, things he won't let himself imagine, and the village is ignorant of them. An unwitting daily reminder delivered in tight, ungenerous faces. His disappointment surges into anger. He is not allowed to be truthful. He is a liar.

Every day, customers tell him that, of course, *men like that* are born liars, untrustworthy, effeminate, weak. Light in their loafers, shirtlifters, nancies, benders. *Men like that* are a menace. Buggers. Keep children safe, boys away. Abusers. Corruptors. Perverts.

Sooner shoot their sons than father *men like that*, meting out shame in everlasting fire. Sinners, sodomites, unnatural and debased. Papers shout of abominations, a disease, a cancer, a terror, a time-bomb, a plague, of *men like that* swirling in the cesspit of their own making. *Men like that* are grossly indecent. *Men like that* should be locked up, hung, stuck, castrated. Every day the customers tell M, this *man like that*.

A piano doesn't pick its tune. So, he will be a liar.

The shop-door of home bells to the evening, he throws the bolt. He stands in the silence. *New Year Sale!* signs and stock and the pulse of coloured fairy lights in the window.

In this slow disco, M takes his boots off, pulls muddy jeans from damp legs, and drops them to the shop floor. He smells aftershave, not his, on his cord jacket. Keen, cheap and sweet. His stomach jumps with excitement.

He thinks of the plateau. He wonders how close they dare go toward an edge before it might crumble and they might fall.

Through flyscreen ribbons he trips up the narrow stairs, holding his half scrap of foolscap and a square of yellow cellophane.

He strips and washes, drops his head to the sink to get the dirt from his hair. Water clouds pink. A cold-weather nosebleed runs over his top lip into his mouth.

Plugs of toilet-roll stopper the iron tang of salty blood. His dad swore blind that stout causes nosebleeds. He feels a wave of love and smiles in contentment from a wonky jaw.

From here, at the foot of the hill, the shadow climbs as the last rays of sun reach higher. A warmer glow. M opens the skylight and the early evening drops cold air past his body like fabric.

He watches until the peak gently lights like a candle.

Cracked/Duck

Daniel Patrick Strogen

Shhh. It's alright. Hush now, love. Now you put your head in by there, that's right. And think of hands that are warm and soft. That's it. You feel my belly going in and out, in and out. I feel your chest going up and down, up and down. Yes, yes. I tell you what. I'll tell us a little story, eh? Would that make it better? Would that take it away? Maybe that's what brought it back. Who knows? Maybe it'll bring it back again. Let's see. Yes, yes. Three glossy birds fly overhead on the sky-blue paper. Quiet as the sin, they drift by beautifully. A hateful sun spits down on the miles of soft, pale, hot sand. All is still. Except for the swaying long grass, yellowed by the fury of God's gaze. Push the sand and see the sea. That is what you see: a perfect day. It's all so beautiful; so clear, so bright, so perfect, it hurts your eyes just to look at it. Look by there. Someone cuts across the sand. There's lovely. In't she pretty? Her eyes are to the floor, yours are at her back. Ah, yes. Yes, yes, yes. She has pretty blonde hair, and she wears a pretty blue dress. You see that material? It's good. Watch it loosen and tighten, loosen and tighten across her shoulders as she walks. Underneath, her arms are thin like a chicken's. Her walk's a bit funny, in't it? She's frantic and frayed. No shape to her. She sees the waves. They clamber and tumble over each other like hungry eager friends. She wants the water to hug her, to fill her up and wash it off, wash it out, the faces, the eyes, and the searing guilt. The sea shushes her bleating. Side-to-side, her head lolls as if she is talking to someone.

Oh yes, a fleeting voice. What she say? Didn't hear her? Did you? Finally, we see her face. The pretty girl smiles a pretty smile. A sad smile. She feels songbirds flutter in her hair. Shhh. Don't the sea just look perfect?

Without you. Summer went and the smog blanketed the town. It crept up the mountains and lingered around the chimney pots. It suffocated the streetlamps and drifted under the doorways. It sweetened, foul and damp, on the tongues of workmen, the mammys and little boys and girls who ran down Church Street. Yes. And nothing grew. Still can't grow nothing round here. Well, nothing good. The smog smothers the seedlings and stirs its nasty fingers in the soil making that nasty too. Every night Hefina said a prayer that was so quiet even she didn't hear it. You know. She laid back and closed her eyes and prayed for rain or sun. Rain brings life, sun riles life, but smog only kills it. Hefina prayed for rain and for sun, for yellow, and green, and red. Hefina prayed that the smog would sink away and spare her paradise.

Hefina lived on Victoria Street. Just there on the corner. That's right, yes, the one that looks like it used to be a shop. With the funny window. Over the years, Hefina had slowly given up that house. Brick by brick, room by room, spoon to spoon. Hefina gave it all up. Gave up all that shit. Except, of course, for the ducks. Hefina didn't know who the house belonged to now. It had been hers at first. The dirty walls, the crooked windowsills, the chipped plant pots, and that dusty shelf, Hefina made her own. Each step she cleaned. Every wall she scrubbed. Every teeny tiny little corner that skinny nothing of a girl stuffed, decorated, painted, and filled with her own. But then James filled it with his love. Whatever that meant. And he took it all for himself. He ate it all up. He swallowed

Hefina too, and the kids. Swallowed them down like a bitter pill. Every face, every pair of eyes, every voice, and every moment. And so, Hefina just gave it all up. And now he had got her garden. But was it James's little self? Or was it something else, something beyond James?

Mrs Awbrey was the one that taught Hefina how to push her love into things. *Arrange them tins. Your favourite Mrs Tom comes on Tuesday mornings.* Hefina loved to do this. All the tins had been hers to look after. To wipe clean, polish and kiss better. Hefina loved it even more when Mrs Tom would turn up, with her unscuffed shoes, untorn tights, and well-combed hair. Mrs Tom would buy two tins of Bully's Best and a sack of apples. And she'd look down at Hefina and her big green eyes would whisper to her. *What a decent, clean girl! And look at that face. In the pictures she could be!* That set Hefina apart from the other kids – the ones who scuffed their shoes, stole their cigarettes, and knocked and ran.

But a lot of time showed Hefina that the adults never really spoke to her. Not Mrs Tom, and not even Mrs Awbrey. They never gave their words; their warm, toasty breath, their wagging tongues, or their big silly teeth. They only gave their eyes to listen to. Come Here, Put That Down, Go To Bed, Take This. You're Just a Girl. But more often than not their eyes were just too quiet and Hefina couldn't hear what they were saying. What you say? I can't hear you. When that happened, that little girl looked in their eyes, saw only herself. Look At That Floor.

Hefina gave up the cigarettes, the tins, the apples, and the house. Now she had to give up the garden. Spuds, leeks, goosegogs, radishes, and big juicy onions. Cuppa tea. Bit of bread and ham. A nice fat onion just pulled out the ground. She'd bring it to her lips and let it all drip down her chin. Then she'd kiss it. Perfect. When the kids were kids, she'd boil whatever good she grew. She'd slice it, chop it, mash it, or mix it up nice and hot with sugar. That was the good thing to do. That was a thing without guilt. But now the garden was sad, faded, grey, gloomy, grotty, and tiny. Just like the house. And Hefina lived there anyway, not because she wanted to. But because she was old and poor. Hefina lived there, surrounded by the smog.

Hefina stood in the front room. Her back and shoulders were hunched and crooked like a cwtched-up little bird. Everyone looked at Hefina like she was ugly and old. She was old, but she knew she weren't ugly. Her back was wrong, her hair was white and nasty, and her face was drawn with lines and grooves. But she knew there was something still pretty about it all. In the mirror, Hefina saw her nany's face. And in her hair, she saw nested robins. And in her back, she saw an old tree. A tree bent and bowed and blown to the side by time. Trees, especially the imperfect ones, were always beautiful to Hefina. She could rub her hands on them, feel the bumps and grooves, and know she was safe now.

But Hefina stood there. And stared. See.

On one wall was her mother-in-law's old clock. Tick, tick, tick, tick, tick, tick. On another were photos of all the kids and grandkids. Yes. That was a good thing to do. On another was the window, and the smog pressing hard against it. Like a begging dog.

On the fourth wall were the ducks.

Three ducks taking flight, pulling themselves out of the fog and into the perfect day. Pushing through the thickness like pushing through a dream, she thought. Hefina only stared at the ducks. Her eyes glistened, dark and fierce. The duck in the middle was cracked. Yes. Right there. A solid, handsome white crack right down the middle. Oh, yes. Hefina looked at it, and it looked right back at her. Tick, tick, tick, tick, tick, tick. Tick.

Angela: Now these were the dancers representing the northeast well there is absolutely no one better we could ask to judge this section than five time world professional Latin American dance champions Danny Hurt and Karen Fairweather What do you think about this makeup and these costumes Danny It's pretty terrific is it not?

Danny: It is tremendous the amount of actual hard work and effort put into them, isn't it, Karen?

Karen: oh yes

Angela: What did you think about tonight's performances?

Danny: Well, we think that with the brilliance of Michael Jackson in both his dancing and his singing that you can't really go wrong. I think they've done a superb job. While on the other hand, the northeast had so many people – we could see it from above – doing such diverse choreography which was so difficult and all part of a central theme. So, it's very difficult to judge –

Angela: Difficult to judge but obviously you had to so how have you portioned the points?

Danny: Here we go. We're giving midlands and west five points and the northeast four points. Isn't that right, Karen?

Karen: oh yes

Angela: Well that means that the score so far in the competition looks like this the midlands and west team have thirteen points and the northeast have eight points well now we move on to the fourth section of our competition which is the old time and we begin with mam the lovely Lola dancing the tango and dancing for midlands an west we have Lola West and Marc Crossley and for Mam Michael Havering MAM Rachel Simpson MAM

'Mam?'

'Yes, love?'

'Are you alright?'

'Yes, love.'

Hefina did not have any money. But with her garden, she was a rich woman. But now her prayers had not been answered. Instead, her big love was the telly. Never really bothered with it before. Now, she ate it all up. In the glare of the television, the two women's eyes were lit up – hungry and lusting. Sat in their housecoats they longed for the gowns blazed into their eyes. They watched them, prancing and turning, dipping and twisting with the music. Hefina could not bear to take her eyes away.

'Ooo, I like hers.'

'Yeah, lovely, in't it.'

They were in the kitchen. Boxes all around them. Hefina was sat, one of her good towels around her shoulders, and her rollers in her hair. Her eldest, Cora, was stood behind her, fiddling gently with the rollers.

'I remember when I used to do your hair, you know?'

Cora tittered but didn't say anything.

'Used to brush it out for hours. God, it was pretty. Long and blonde. And then, I'd tie it up with a lovely little ribbon. Do you remember that, Cora?'

'Yeah,' Cora only said.

A little while later, their hair permed, the two ladies were at the kitchen table.

'There's egg on that, Mam.'

'Pass it here.'

'When they coming over tomorrow, then?'

Tick, tick, tick, tick, tick, tick.

'First thing. Nine o'clock,' Hefina answered.

'There we are then. That's good. You can put your feet up in the evening, then.'

'I don't know how the bloody hell they're going to get that cupboard downstairs. Needs chucking really.'

'Mam!' Cora twisted her face with exaggerated outrage. 'You can't go leaving that out for the gypsies. That was Nany's, weren't it?'

'No, mun. That was your *father's* mother's.'

'Oh right. Well, I'm sure if they just—'

'Ugly *fucking* thing.'

Tick, tick, tick, tick, tick, tick.

'I worry about you, mind.'

'Oh, shut up, mun. I'm an old woman, not a little girl.'

Hours later the old woman was cocooned in her duvet. The space behind her was free, but she never took it. If it was up to her, she and James wouldn't have shared a bed. In the early years of her marriage, she would wake up with James on top of her. His chin rough against her forehead. His breath stinking. So many times, she had pretended to fall asleep at Iona's next door. A few times she had gone downstairs. Her feet soft as feathers on the wooden steps. No creaking, no cracking. And she'd find him asleep on the kitchen floor. That was a real treat. She'd just look at him, broken on the floor. She wouldn't stop looking at him, like the way new mothers can't stop looking at their new-borns. She'd look at him for hours. Feel the poison and the hate rushing around in her mouth. *Maybe some of that hate was for me too.* She'd give him a sharp kick. He wouldn't wake up.

Tick, tick, tick, tick, tick, tick. TICK.

Hefina did not get up right away. She was enjoying the quiet. Nobody appreciated the quiet like Hefina. *Sometimes silence is the best music there is.*

Nancy had let herself in, and the boys had joined her a few minutes later. She could hear their low voices moving about the room below her. Nancy was cooing away in her mother's voice. Giving them orders, moving boxes of teacups and clattering with pans.

'God, you're a fucking twat, mind.'

'Never mind that. I'll chuck the kettle on, you go and get some hobnobs.'

'God, this place is a tip —'

'Hush up, mun. She'll hear you.'

'Where is she then? Not still asleep is she?'

Then the door knocked.

'Mam?'

Hefina didn't turn. She didn't want to look at her daughter. Not yet.

'Mam?'

Hefina pretended to be asleep. She might leave her be for a bit then.

'Mam.'

Hefina turned and yawned.

'Oh sorry, flower,' she said softly. 'I must have overslept. Are the boys here yet?'

'Yeah, come on. Give yourself a quick wash and I'll give you a hand with getting dressed.'

Hefina made herself look her youngest in the face. God, she was young. Her face was full and fresh. Like a lovely fat, round apple. Hefina could think about the girls and Michael like that now. *You can't give yourself beauty. Someone's got to give it to you.* That's what Hefina said to Nancy when she had come home one night, her new white eyeliner smudged. Oh, how the kids were beautiful. James had never given Hefina beauty. For a long time, she thought James had infected her. Whenever she thought about the kids. Their fine blonde hair, or their delicate pretty pale skin. She knew, truly, that she didn't want them. But she still felt that lurking within her veins. James had taken beauty away from her.

Tick, Tick, Tick, Tick, Tick, Tick. TICK.

By midday, there wasn't much else left. Most of it deserved the tip anyway. And it was easy for Hefina to see it thrown away. Hefina drifted into the living room when Nancy buttered a few slices of white. The boys had a cuppa and smoked whilst they kicked their heels out the front.

It was all gone. Except for the ducks. Hefina looked at the crack. The thin, slim white line.

The ducks are on the floor in the kitchen.

The table is overturned.

Someone is whimpering.

James is gone. But he comes back. And he does it again. And again. You heard that, didn't you? You knew.

'Mam! Have you been hiding ham again?' Nance cawed. Hefina found her knees were weak.

'Mam!'

Hefina dropped herself into the only chair left in the room.

'Mam!'

'It's under the stairs!' Hefina answered, still staring at the duck. Waiting for it to fall, hit the ground and shatter across the floor.

'Dozy, stupid bitch, you are,' James said, a tight hand around her neck, another clutching a handful of her thin, blonde hair. 'What do you fucking do all day? Eh? Can't even cook a bit of fucking meat right.'

'Mam, you alright?'

'You hear about Mary – moving to Canada, with wassisname Keith, in't it?' Hefina called out, refusing to take her gaze away from the duck. Go on, drop and crack.

'Yeah, Cora told me the other day.'

'Yeah, she's moving to Canada with Keith. Don't like it round here, too limiting apparently. I said June was having problems with that girl. Blue nail polish, in't it? Pain in the arse she is.'

'Well, if she wants to go, let her go,' Nancy said.

'She can go – but she'll be back before long. I'm telling you. I'm no shunk! she says. I said, you fuck off to Canada and leave the rest of us to take care of your mam.'

'She has to make herself happy, Mam.'

'No. You have to be good for your kids, first. For your mammy. *Then* for yourself, love.'

'Eat your sandwich, Mam,' Nancy said a little too sharply, shoving a plate into Hefina's hand. Hefina looked at the sandwich on her plate. She lifted the top and examined the ham. Pink and slick.

'That's the ham I give to the kids. The good ham's under the stairs.'

Nancy's thin lips became even thinner.

'For God's sake, Mam!'

TICK TICK TICK TICK TICK TICK TICK.

A little while later and the boys were gone. Nancy and Hefina were leaving by the front door. Crossing the doorway for the last time. Nancy felt little for that house, but Hefina felt even less. Yet, for some reason she lingered behind.

'You coming, Mam?' Nancy asked, her words edged with concern.

'Just going to stay for a bit.'

'Why, what you going to do?'

'Don't worry about what I'm going to do. I'll see you outside now.'

Nancy let a comical sigh fill up the room and shut the door behind her.

There she was. Hefina. All alone in a house that wasn't hers. She saw them still. No one had gone near them. Christ they smacked. Even from here, she could smell them. Smacked of the poison that had been pumped into them. Cora and Nancy had left them alone. Why was that? Did they remember? Or maybe they just felt it. The boys had left them alone. Maybe they were too scared of the pure evil that clung to them.

Hefina faced them. She reached up. She stretched up her fingers and let herself feel them. They were delicate. The smoothness, the twisted kindness of them, was too much to bear.

That's right. I've come in from the shop. Got myself a new pair of tights. Oh, and a nice couple of daffodils. They'll look pretty on the windowsill. The duck is on the floor. Broken in half, right down its body. The table is overturned. In the corner, Michael is whimpering. Holding two red palms up to Heaven. But I hold myself back. Yes, stop myself from touching him, from looking into his eyes. If I do that, it is real. Everything I knew is real. But he looks into my eyes and sees my fear and guilt. Isn't it just, Mam? And he takes it to heart. Right to his little heart it went. And he kept it there forever. Bless him. Did I leave him there? I followed the breadcrumbs, the evil of how they got there plain as day. The evil that now occupied those things: the torn socks, the shoe with the snapped buckle, the ribbon on the top step. The split duck in the kitchen. Sprawled on the floor of the landing, asleep, was little Cora. Unconscious. Her dress torn and ruffled and bloodied. I had laid it out for her. Pretty daisies on it. Now the daisies were stained. I saw her pale, thin little legs. I could have smacked the shit out of them. Why did you let it happen? You knew what he was like. Why? I could have whipped and slapped them until the skin was red. I wanted to pick her up and hold her and cry for her and cry for Michael, for little James and for myself. Snap! I went. Just like a chicken bone. Shhh. There she is. The broad sea in front of her. A bowlful of blue. You see her there? Did that make it better? Did that take it away? Hmm? It was a perfect day when I flew. Flew away from the smog. I thought about taking it with me. I also thought about smacking it off the wall and bellowing and crying as it shattered around me. But I lowered my hand. I left it there. Like a ghost it could wait and die. I locked the door behind me and reminded myself to post the keys through the letterbox. I'd miss my little garden. My little patch of paradise. Maybe I can make another one once the smog sinks away.

Hefina left the house and locked the door behind her. Nancy was waiting by the car for her – her arms all crossed and eyebrows up in that Are You Going To Tell Me What's Going On Or What kind of way.

No, no, no. I don't think so.

'How's Michael getting on with that grouting, then?' she asked her daughter.

Shhh. The silence is perfect.

Splott Elvis and the Sundance Kid

Lindsay Gillespie

Early one morning. Midges and diesel. It's 6.15. The boy looks up at the sky. Just the one cloud up there, which sort of looks like a chicken leg. And a dried-up lump of sun that, today of all days, is acting like it really can't be arsed.

It's all wrong. He wants a summer sun today, a monster sun, the colour of electric Lucozade. He wants this day to feel different. He needs a sign. He left a note on the kitchen table when he walked out an hour ago. He's walked a mile and three quarters to junction 26. And it's already going wrong; the one thing he needs, he's gone and left on the table. He slips into the motorway services and finds what he's after. A packet of magic markers. He pulls out a pound to pay, but the pen doesn't have a price on it.

'H-how m-m-m...' he goes.

He flaps his head from side to side to shake out the rest of the word, but it's jammed and won't come out.

Little Miss Cutie behind the counter finishes his sentence.

'How much are the magic markers? It's 80p for one, or two for £1.20, and a packet of...'

He's out the shop.

Then he turns around. He has to have the pen; his plan depends on it.

The girl's disappeared down an aisle. Stu stuffs a packet of pens down his jeans and, on the way out, scoops up two Pepsis and a family-size buttercream swiss roll.

His stammer's messed up a lot of things. But it's made him the best shoplifter in the Fourth Form.

Outside he crosses the scabby carpark to check he's on the right side of the M4. He's heading out west. Or is it north. Whatever, he needs a sign. This close to the motorway feels like a warzone. Forty-four-tonne dragons whumping past. He gets down on his knees to pick through some brambles. Nappies, licked out milkshake carton. Then he finds it, the other thing he's after. An old crisp box. A-B-E-R he writes on it, in serial killer letters. That's half the word. The letter A is already bleeding off the box.

He looks up. Now there's a whole bunch of the chicken legs in the sky. The biggest one squirts him right in the eye. Splat. It's gobbing rain.

A lorry honks.

'Saying your prayers down there?'

He hasn't even stuck his thumb out yet.

A voice with an elasticky twang in it.

'So where to you heading?'

Stu scrabbles for his crisp box.

'Cheese and Onion?'

'A-a-aber...'

He knew his stammer would mess up his plan, it's why he had to have a sign.

'Aber. But which one? You got Aberaeron and Aberdare. There's Aberdulais, Aberthin, Aberdeilo, Aberporth, Abertillery. Plus Aberkenfig, Abercarn, Abergele, Aberystwyth...'

'Aber. Ab-b-b bercynon?' Stu's no longer sure that's the one he's heading for. He wishes the driver hadn't recited all the others.

'Not my route, but reckon I can get you close enough. Hop in.'

Stu clambers up the silver steps.

'Pardonnez le pigsty.' The driver shoos the herd of cans off the passenger seat. Stu sits down. The cab is hot and crowded. There's posters and photos all around the windscreen.

'Th…thanks for g-giving me a lift. My name's… I'm S-Stu.'

The driver turns to face him.

'No prize for guessing mine,' grins the driver.

Stu has no idea what he's on about.

Hairy nose, sticking-out teeth, sweat raining down his cheeks. Stu runs through his mam's record collection: Ken Dodd? Englebert Humperdinck?

The driver nods at the banner stretched across the windscreen spelling out five letters in blue glitter.

Ah, okay then. Though Stu reckons his mam's Jack Russell, Hoppit, looks more like Elvis Presley than this guy. One thing for sure he's got is Elvis hair; his quiff is like black jelly. Plus the spiky-toed cowboy boots, and a shirt with silver horseshoes on. These things, plus the twang makes Stu wonder out loud:

'S-so, you from America?'

'Couldabeen,' says the driver, 'shouldabeen. Every day I ask the man above, what the Bo Diddly?'

'What the Bo d-diddly what?'

'What I'm doing here.'

'In Malpas?'

'Talking about Cardiff.'

'What about Cardiff?'

'I'm referring more to Splott, as it happens.'

'What's with S-splott?'

'Overcrowded. Can't move for Elvises in Splott. Everyone

and their dog thinks they're Elvis.' The driver winds down the window and spits out into the rain. 'Time for me to move on.'

'Bristol? London?'

The driver takes a look at Stu. 'You're a kid. You've got the small-town thinking going on. Got to think big.'

'Tokyo,' says Stu. Biggest city in the world. They did it last term with Mr Bowen.

The driver flips his quiff.

'Memphis, Tennessee. Elvis HQ.'

There's a pause.

'Wow. Won't there b-be like a million Elvis fans there though?'

'How many Welsh Elvises though?'

There's a lull in the cab. The cans dinging under Stu's chair have stopped. He's using his feet like brakes. To muffle them.

'There's this boy at school,' says Stu, 'he went to America last year.'

'Yeah? Was he knocked out by it?'

'Said it was alright. Said they eat a lot.'

'That it? That all he say?'

'Yeah. No. He said they call tramps b-bums, and he said you can get b-bread in a tin can.'

'Wowser,' Splott Elvis spins the wheel, 'that kid, I'd whup his you-know-what. I wouldn't go sending a nincompoop like that out the house for a pint of milk, never mind to the US of A.'

Stu shuts up. Splott Elvis is making him twitchy. He considers his situation. He knows you're meant to earn your ride. He knows sweet FA about Mr E. P. He remembers his shoplifting.

'Want a P...Pepsi?'

Splott Elvis laughs.

'Hear that?'

A bit of speed and the cans come loose and start going at each other again under the seats.

'Take a wild guess what I got in the back of the lorry,' says Splott Elvis. 'You're riding the Pepsi Express. Seventy-five crates back there.'

Stu blinks.

'Can you drink them for free? How many Pepsis do you get through a day then?'

'To be honest they give me windypops these days. Elvis is a twenty-can-a-day man, so they say. God knows how he manages it. He's also partial to a black cherry soda, which you can't get in this country for love nor money.'

More rain now. Stu looks out at the muffled motorway. This whole summer's been rubbish.

'So, what's the w-weather like,' Stu pipes up, 'where Elvis lives?'

'Average Memphis summer day? You're looking at 90 degrees. Got the sun shining out their arse 24/7 over there. Can you imagine?'

He looks over at Stu.

'No, you can not.'

The lorry goes whump and the cans pogo.

'How do you know so much? You in the Elvis fan club?'

'Check this out.' Splott Elvis points at the floor by his pedals. Fanzines.

He flings a few over. *Elvis Close Up*, *Memphis Rock*, *Elvis Special*.

'All American. Special order.'

The can of Pepsi goes flying and Splott Elvis smacks his horn.

'Mother...' he yanks down the window, '...fucker!'

Splott Elvis cuts up a Ford Cortina and a minivan.

Stu shuts his eyes. Splott Elvis is the horriblest driver.

He spins the wheel.

'Been on the road last two days. Feeling dead as a dog, so your job, Stu, if you'll accept it, is to help me out.'

Stu eyes him. He has decided he'll be polite, but first chance, he's legging it. He'll have to do it sooner rather than later, preferably while he's still alive.

'You got to talk, keep me going.'

Stu's more of a listener than a talker. The stammer sees to that.

'Or I'll drop off at the wheel. Has been known. My last two lorries were a write-off.'

Jeez.

'How's about you ask me coupla questions? Like *Mastermind*. You know my specialist subject. Right, so the clock's ticking.'

Stu's a blank.

'Where, where d-does Elvis live, for real? You know, like the a-actual address?'

Best he can think of.

'It's a ten-hour flight to Miami International, and a two-hour hop to Memphis. Twelve miles south of downtown Memphis gets you to Highway 51. Then it's five minutes to Elvis Presley Boulevard Number 3764. Boom! Next one!'

'I, I, I…'

'Come on, we only just got going!'

' W-what does Elvis drive?'

'Nice one. So he's got a '72 Fleetwood Thunderbird,' Splott Elvis is off, 'a Stutz Blackhawk, a Tomaso Pantera.'

Stu takes a little mini break and looks out the window. They've turned off the motorway now and there are fields and trees. They make the rain look green.

'And he's got the 1960 Silver Cloud, the Ferrari Dino. There was this time when the Ferrari, it doesn't want to start, so he pulls out a gun and shoots it.'

'Woo, that s-sounds…' like Elvis is a bit of a dick, Stu wants to say.

'But if I had to sum up his taste in cars? One word. Cadillacs. Owns two hundred and fifty of them. One time he bought thirty-two before breakfast. Dishes them out like candy. Most every girl he dates gets a Caddy.'

This clues Stu in with the next question.

'And what's the n-name of his girlfriend?'

'Lady he's with now? That would be Miss Ginger Alden.'

'I was thinking when he was younger, l-like my age.'

'The Brunette from Biloxi, Miss Dixie Loxie. Or Locke it is really. They dated early '53 till…'

Stu sneaks a look at his watch. He's not going to make the festival. Elvis catches him looking.

'My turn now. I'll ask the questions. You're what, sixteen, seventeen?'

Stu nods. He was fourteen last January.

'You running away? Off skylarking with your buds? Maybe planning a Thunderbird party or two?'

Stu shakes his head.

'I'm going to this festival.'

'Who's playing?'

'It's not a music one.'

'How do you mean?'

'It's called SpiritFest.'

'Hippie, is it?'

'Don't think so. It's for p-pp people who want to ch-change. If you go, you can get help.'

'Help from who?'

'The Holy S-spirit.'
Splott Elvis slows right down.

Diggory Degweed has promised Stu on his mam's life he'll get him into SpiritFest. Diggory and him are in the same class at St Teilo's, but in different social groups. Stu's group is Rob, Gobbo, Bryn. Diggory's social group is Diggory. The boys and the teachers still call him the new boy, though he's been at school for over a year. His name hasn't helped. Gobbo was the first to call him Deadweed. Nor the fact he used to go to some poncey school, and he's cricket and rowing, and St Teilo's is footie and rugby. What's tricky is Deadweed's new house, it's a heartbeat from Stu's. He lingers so they can walk together. Stu will walk the first bit, but he's dead if the others spot him with Diggory. His old name Stuttering Stu has sort of petered out. Hanging with Deadweed would be fresh ammo.

Mr Bowen delivers whiny play-nice speeches at registration. 'Come on lads. Include every boy when you're picking teams.' By which he means Diggory. It's just more fun not to. There was one home time when Mr Bowen made one of his Special Announcements. 'Calling all Subbuteo fans,' he said. 'A new after-school club this Friday, boys. 4.30 to 6.00pm. 27, Coed Glas.' Diggory's house. The following Monday Diggory told him not a single boy showed up. Stu said he'd been on his way, but his mam had tripped over the dog, and banged her knee.

Then everything changed. You couldn't open a paper without seeing pictures of this girl with wide-apart green eyes and ripply hair. Diggory's sister, Bella. Interviews, magazines, Breakfast TV, she popped up everywhere to tell her story. The story was that in the middle of 'Giselle' – Bella's a ballet dancer – she went blind. She leapt off stage, and smashed up her ankles.

Then last summer, someone told her about SpiritFest. She went. She asked for help. Got her sight back on the spot, she said. Wasn't just her, Diggory had told them in the playground. This kid with a withered leg – it grew two inches! And this old miner, he'd had the shakes for thirty years. They just stopped. An associated mini-miracle was Diggory. He's Mr Popular now. And Stu's the lurker, hanging about to walk to school with Digg. He's been asking him for help. This summer his stammer's been skidding about worse than ever. Diggory knows what Stu's after. In a pleasurable show of benevolence, he says he thinks he might be able to get him into the sold-out festival.

'You a Bible basher then?'

'Christmas and Easter. When my nan takes me.'

'My gramps was a preacher man. Bethel Baptist. One Sunday he's in the pulpit, opens the Bible, bangs it shut, and walks out.'

'W-what'd he do that for?'

'He said reading the Bible was like reading the back of a packet of cornflakes. But the cornflakes box was more interesting.'

Splott Elvis starts to speed up.

'Let's have us a song. You pick.'

Stu flicks through the cassettes. 'They all Elvis?'

'Duh.'

'But if you wanted to listen to someone else, like just for a change?'

'Never gonna happen. You got the lot with Elvis. Gospel? Tick. Country, rock? Tick, tick. Hillbilly? Elvis, again. Don't even have a radio anymore. Only distracts me.'

The lorry kangaroo-hops as Splott Elvis switches lanes.

'Who you a fan of?'

'David B-b-bowie.' Stu's big brother's a Bowie freak.

'Bowie's okay. Want to know how come?'

'How c-come.'

'Same birthday as Mr E.P. Which is…?'

Stu puts on a squinty fake-remembering face.

'January,' Elvis helps him out.

'Can't r-remember exact…'

'Jeez. The eighth. January the eighth.' Splott Elvis takes a corner too fast. 'That's the difference, see, between righteous fans like me, and half-arsed ones like…'

'O-okay, but I only just got into him.'

'So what's your favourite Bowie song, then?'

''Ch-ch-changes'.'

Elvis laughs.

'Know how many songs Elvis has done? Four hundred, give or take. How many number ones?'

'N-no idea.'

'Eighteen. Know them all off by heart. Go on, test me.'

This again. Test me, test me. Stu was stuck, all the way to Aber-whatever with this nutter.

''Hound Dog'. That sold four million.'

Stu's eyes were closing, 'Wow, that's am-am…' he's jammed up. They jump a pothole and the stuck-together words in Stu's throat hurtle out, '…mazing. That's amazing.'

'I know all the lyrics, every word. You can test me,' says Splott Elvis, 'go on.'

'I d-don't…'

'Inside the cassettes. I copied out all the lyrics.'

Stu shovels through the cassettes. He slips in 'The Wonder of You'.

A trilling intro. Then the blend of Elvis Elvis and Splott Elvis together with the swell of rain outside, and the Pepsi cans dinging away makes it a very metal version. Splotty is word-perfect. His voice is rich and stirring. No trace of an accent, Stu notices, neither Splott nor yankee.

Next one up: 'Peace in the Valley'.

It's like Stu is the audience in a private festival and Elvis is singing just for him.

'You know you sing b-b-br...you're a great singer.'

Splott Elvis really is.

'I get a load of practice.'

The cab blitzes with a cold silver light.

'That lightning?' asks Stu.

The lorry wobbles.

An ambulance siren cries off to the left.

'Thing is,' Splotty Elvis roars over it, 'you do this job, you get lonely. Elvis sings to me, and I sing back.'

More sirens now.

'I talk to him, tell him stuff.'

Elvis's arm is sticking out of the open window, blistered with rain.

'Not being funny, but you ever tried singing for your speech thing?'

'F-for my stammer? They made me go to this c-clinic. I had to s-sing baby songs. They got me to talk to myself in a m-mirror. And do d-dumb tongue-twisters. Red l-lorry, yellow l-lorry. Mam said if anything m-my stammer was getting way worse. In the end I j-just stopped going.'

'When was this?'

'Five years back.'

The lorry skids, and Elvis is driving like a banshee, they're hurtling towards a bridge that's come from nowhere, and Stu is flung against the windscreen, getting pelted by the cans.

At the last second, Elvis swerves clear.

'My dose!' cries Stu.

He fingers it. There's a sprinkle of blood on his fingers.

'You just d-dusted my dose!'

Splotty glances over.

'It's just your lip.'

'You went straight for the b-b-bridge!'

'Sorry, sorry. Thought it might help.'

'Break my n-nose?' says Stu. 'That helps me how?'

'The stammer. I read about this kid in one of the Elvis mags. This dog jumped up and bit this kid's cheek. Never stammered before, now the boy's stammering nonstop. Worse than you. Family tries everything, and everything doesn't work. Kid stammering 24/7. They see this specialist, that specialist. Then one day they're at the supermarket, and the checkout girl sees the problem. She tells the mam this secret cure. That night the mam fills the bath with ice. When the kid's fast asleep, she tips him in. Three nights in a row she does it. Kid never ever stammers again. Shock for a shock they call it.'

Stu nibbles the blood off his bottom lip.

'I call it b bollocks. Plus I bet he hated his mam. Like really, really hated her.'

'Sorry about your lip,' says Splott.

Stu ignores him.

Splott's driving carefully now, changing gears quietly.

'Any requests?'

Stu couldn't care less. He's still mad at Splotty.

'Know this one?' Elvis puts in a fresh cassette.

Stu grunts. This song. This is the only Elvis he's heard before. It's the one about the baby and the ghetto and the baby's mam who can't stop crying. Splott Elvis climbs up the chorus, to the high notes. He's drowning out Elvis. Then Elvis is drowning out Splott Elvis. It is the saddest song.

'Mac Davies, 1969. B side is 'Any Day Now'. How about you join in the chorus with me. Just the one time. Might take your mind off that lip.'

The cab is racketing about with the rain and Pepsi cans and there's no way he's going to burst into song to please a lunatic lorry driver. He's spent the last ten years fake-singing in every Christmas concert, every Eisteddfod, every assembly; you name it, he's got by and never sung a single word. Stu opens his mouth, to fake sing. But his voice isn't having it. A note drips out, then another. His throat and his tongue are not fighting him, not at all, not at this moment. The song is noble, melancholic. The thunderstorm crashes in from outside and rearranges the melody.

Elvis takes both hands off the steering wheel, and back slaps Stu.

'You did it! No stammer!'

First time I've sung anything, thinks Stu, since 'She'll Be Coming Round the Mountain'.

They swoop along the A48, the Pepsi cans babbling in the back.

'Reckon there's girls at this festival of yours?' asks Elvis.

Bound to be, thinks Stu. If he gets cured, he's talking to every single one of them. Diggory's sister in particular. Every boy in St Teilo's wants to talk to Bella.

'Girls go mad for Elvis,' says the driver. 'And Elvis girls, I got to tell you, don't take no for an answer.'

Splott Elvis leers and thrashes the gears.

'What else you know about this festival, then?'

'Only what I said.'

'And you heard about it how?'

'This boy at school. His sister went blind, then she went to Spiritfest and got her sight back, 100%.'

'Just like that?'

'Just like that. She was on telly, magazines, everything. Heath Hospital checked her out.'

Splott Elvis bumps softly over a pothole.

'She says she doesn't exactly believe in miracles. She just says this is what happened to her.'

A heavenly blue light fills the cab.

The police car pulls in front of him, sirens on. Stu isn't sure Elvis is going to brake. Waves of blue rain swirl across the windscreen. He brakes, and pulls up in a lay-by.

'Fuck,' says Elvis, '...fucky fuck fuck.'

The policewoman approaches, and raps on the window.

'Licence please, sir.'

'Here you go,' Splott Elvis winks at Stu, and passes it to her, 'dollface.'

'Why you calling her that?' Stu hisses.

'They like it. The ladies.'

'Could you please step out of the vehicle, sir.'

The policewoman has just spotted Stu.

'And you are?'

'I'd like to present, ma'am, my junior partner in crime,' says Splott Elvis, 'the Sundance Kid!'

The policewoman's mouth snaps to a slit.

'Sir?'

'Only joking you.'

'You've been recorded as driving without due care and attention. That means I can issue you with a fine on the spot.'

'You could, lovely lady, but I'm guessing you won't.'

'How's that, sir?'

Splott Elvis nods over at the patrol car.

The car door is open, and there's a jangle of noise; over the

161

crackle of the walkie talkie, the sobbing chorus of 'Always On My Mind' is just building to a crescendo.

'A woman with very good taste. Think we might have something in common.' Splott Elvis does his leer face again.

The policewoman looks back at the squad car. 'It's been Elvis all morning. The radio hasn't let up since the news came in. Of course, there's the time difference. It happened yesterday afternoon. They're saying it was his heart.'

Splott Elvis stares at her. He stumbles, his legs get tangled up in each other. Then he's off, streaking past the police car. Heading for the road.

There's a policeman in the car, he's up and chasing Splott Elvis. Elvis loops back and flies past the lorry. Past the litterbins, up into the bushes.

The policewoman comes around to Stu's side of the lorry, and looks around the cab.

'Your dad a big fan, then? Oh yes, I can see that now.'

'He's the n-number one Elvis f-fan. In Wales.'

'Look, tell your dad, just tell him to take it easy. He's had a big shock. Tell him to drive slow. Fifty up here. Look after him, won't you?'

Stu says he will. The patrol car pulls away.

Stu waits. 7.35 now. Splott Elvis has been up in the brambles for quarter of an hour.

He should go and find him. Stu climbs down. He picks out squashed insect legs from out the windscreen wipers. They stick to his fingers.

A voice behind him.

'Get back in.'

Stu wriggles back up to his seat. Elvis's face is yellow. His shirt's splattered. And something else. No black quiff. His head is speckled with freckles.

Stu doesn't dare ask what's happened to Splotty's hair.

Splott Elvis sits in his seat with his head stuck to the steering wheel.

Stu waits a bit, then passes him the giant swiss roll.

Splott Elvis takes a bite, tosses it out the window.

'Got a cigarette?'

Stu shakes his head.

'That policewoman. She say it was for sure. No mistake?'

Stu shrugs.

Splott's nose is running down his shirt, in and out of the silver horseshoes.

'Got to go home. Think you could drive me?'

Stu stares at him.

'N-not really. I c-can't drive.'

Splotty revs the engine.

'Sorry, but I'll be leaving you here, if that's okay. You're not a million miles from your Aber. Not a bad spot to catch a lift.'

True, thinks Stu. It's not bad, it's a nightmare.

'What you doing?' asks Stu halfway down the steps.

'Turning around. Heading for home. Can't take it in.' Elvis lifts his face from the wheel. 'Forty-two. Same as me. All the best, Stu. Hope you make it.'

Elvis throws the lorry in reverse, zigzags a little, and pulls out, just missing a school bus. A snarl of horns, and he's away.

Stu stands there. His crisp-box sign is in the lorry, under the passenger seat.

Splott's a bit of a motherfucker, to be honest, dumping him amongst these thornbushes, amongst the smell of dead things. Middle of nowhere. Nothing to drink or eat. Things could be worse, mind. The lorry hadn't crashed. The police hadn't arrested him, or found out his age, where he lived and phoned his mam. And the rain looks like it's thinking about stopping.

And now he'll stammer for the rest of his life.

He thinks about the Holy Spirit. The girls he'll never talk to.

He sees something in the brambles. Something dead or dying. Something hit by a car, that's crawled in here to die. He nudges it with his trainer. Splotty's wig.

A voice. Someone's calling him.

'Oi! Said I'd get you where you're going. Get in before I go changing my mind.'

'Thanks.' Stu's seat is still warm. 'You're still going to Memphis though, to his house and everything?'

Splott shakes his head. 'Not without him there, I'm not.'

'I could c-come with you. If you like.'

Splott Elvis grunts. Stu has Splott's wig in his lap, he's patting it like it's Hoppit. He passes it over, without a word.

Splott Elvis is spinning the wheel. 'Been getting too much, to tell you the truth. Elvis, Elvis, everything Elvis. It was like he'd got inside of me, taken over. Not his fault. I let him. It's been getting out of hand.' Elvis shakes his head. 'Hell time is it?'

'I've missed the festival. It's okay.'

'The Spirit might be minded to hang about. Hang tight. Watch this. Gonna open us a can of whup-ass.'

The lorry rears up. They roar up the A40. Long villages, and tiny ones that seem to run out of themselves before they even begin.

Splott buzzes a sign.

'That say Aber?'

'You're going too fast.'

'There, over there. What's that say. That an Aber?'

Most every sign they're seeing now says Aber something.

'Should have an Aber festival,' says Elvis.

They're bouncing through squeezed-up terraces, straggles of pubs and shut-up shops.

Elvis brakes hard.

'This is,' he announces, 'the last village.'

Stu looks out the window, then at his watch. 8.05.

'We only gone and done it!' Splott is jubilant.

'Now where's the Spirit?'

They pass a lad carrying a crash helmet.

'Know where the festival is?' He turns to Stu. 'The spirit one?'

The lad gives them the finger.

Stu calls out to a woman kicking at a buggy.

'You don't happen to know where the festival is?'

'Nothing happens here,' she says. 'Ever.'

'I got news for you. You've got a massive festival happening on your doorstep.'

She points down the empty street, 'Try The Pony. They know everything.'

The ugly pub takes up what's left of the village.

'Won't be a minute.' Splott swipes his wig off Stu's lap, stuffs it on sideways, changes his mind. Flings it back through the window. The glass doors of The Pony swallow him up.

While he's waiting, Stu pulls down the passenger mirror. He breathes on it, like the lady at the speech clinic showed him.

'Hey there, d-dollface.' His bottom lip has a lump of dark blood on it, like a bogey. He smiles at himself. He pops Splotty's wig on. Tries again.

'Bella, hiya. I'm in the same class as your b-brother. Thought you might like, err, just wondered if you're into David B-bowie?'

He does an astonished look in the mirror.

'No way! Me too. Been into him forever. It's so weird. I've got the same b-b-birthday as him.'

Stu decides to change mirrors. He has a second conversation with Bella, this time in the wing mirror. This one goes even better. He counts just the one stammer the whole time.

When he gets home he's learning every word to the whole of *Aladdin Sane*. He's going to practise till he's word perfect like Splotty. He will so slay Bella Degweed.

He snaps the mirror back. Splott Elvis is just leaving The Pony. He's weaving his way towards the lorry. He stops and looks up. Stu looks too. A huge stretch of blue sky. No chicken leg clouds. And breaking free, a cosmic sun the colour of Fanta.

Splott Elvis opens the back of the van.

'Guess what?' He rips the ring-pulls off two fresh Pepsis.

'Wrong Aber completely.'

Author Biographies

Born in south Wales, **Lindsay Gillespie** now lives in the South Downs. In between she worked in India and Japan. In 2021, she was a Costa Short Story Prize Finalist, shortlisted for Fiction Factory and Oxford Flash Fiction and longlisted for Exeter Short Story Prize. She was interviewed on Storyradio in March 2022 and her stories have also featured on the podcast. She is completing her debut short story collection. Twitter: @LindsGillesp14

Bethan James is a freelance writer and former book publicist from the Vale of Glamorgan. In 2021, she was selected to represent Wales in the United Nations' global feminist fairytale retellings anthology, *Awake Not Sleeping*. Other achievements include: a winner in Neil Gaiman & Word Factory's Fables for a Modern World contest; shortlisted for the Bristol Prize; and published by *Litro Magazine*, among others. Bethan is working on her debut novel represented by DHH Literary Agency. Twitter: @thebethanjames

Meredith Miller grew up in New York and moved to Britain in 1997. She is the author of two published novels, *Little Wrecks* (2017) and *How We Learned to Lie* (2018) as well as several short stories and a body of literary criticism. A Welsh learner, Meredith is an avid reader of Welsh fiction in both English and Cymraeg. She lives in mid Wales and teaches and supervises Creative Writing at Cardiff University. Twitter: @meredithseven

Laura Morris is from Caerphilly. She has an MA in Creative Writing from The University of Wales, Bangor. Her work has been published by Honno Press and broadcast on BBC Radio 4. Recent short stories have appeared in *The Lonely Crowd* and *Banshee*. She lives in Cardiff where she teaches English at a Welsh-medium secondary school. Twitter: @Morris78L

Jonathan Page lives in Bronllys, close to the Black Mountains. He works as a technical author and writes literary fiction in his spare time. His short stories have appeared in six anthologies since 2015, and his story 'Sacrifice' won the Hay Writers Prize in 2018. His first novel, *Blue Woman*, the life story of a fictional Welsh artist, was published in April 2022 by Weatherglass Books. He has written about *Blue Woman* for both *Wales Arts Review* and *New Welsh Review*. Twitter: @JonPage30363996

Matthew G. Rees grew up in the border country known as the Marches in a Welsh family with roots in both industrial and rural Wales. He has – among other things – been a journalist, a teacher and a night-shift cab driver. His first book *Keyhole*, a collection of short stories set in Wales and the Marches, was published in 2019. His most recent book is *The Snow Leopard of Moscow & Other Stories*, a collection of stories set in Putin-era Moscow where Matthew lived and worked for a period prior to a PhD and other studies at Swansea University. Twitter: @ReesMatthewG

Eryl Samuel lives near Cardiff where he was born and brought up. He currently works as a school improvement partner with schools in Rhondda Cynon Taf, Cardiff and the Vale of Glamorgan. His first collection of short stories, *Words are Like Birds*, was published in 2021. He has also written a novel, *Cat's Eyes*, published in 2020. A second volume of short stories is in the pipeline for publication by the end of the year. Twitter: @afoldintheworld

Matthew David Scott is from Manchester, England but made Wales his home some twenty years ago. He is the author of two novels: the Dylan Thomas Prize longlisted *Playing Mercy* (Parthian 2005) and *The Ground Remembers* (Parthian 2009). A founder member of theatre company, Slung Low, Matthew's work has been performed at theatres such as The Barbican, The Almeida, The Everyman, and in fields, car parks and town centres across the U.K. He lives in Newport. Twitter: @scottyslunglow

Carys Shannon is originally from the North Gower in Swansea and now works remotely between Spain and Wales as a digital storyteller and content writer. Carys studied Drama at Aberystwyth University before going on to work as a producer for National Theatre Wales, Volcano Theatre Company and other socially engaged arts projects. In 2017, she graduated from the University of South Wales with an MPhil in Writing, and has had short stories published by Honno Press, Parthian Books and most recently, *Mslexia Magazine*. She is currently finishing her first novel which has been longlisted for the Bath and Mslexia Novel Awards and shortlisted for the Caledonia Novel award. A passionate animals rights advocate and vegan, Carys believes stories have the power to change the world. Twitter: @WriterCarys

Anthony Shapland grew up in Bargoed in the Rhymney Valley. His work, as a writer, artist and filmmaker blends documentary and fiction, building on his sense that the world is constructed in the same way as a film set – constantly evolving and temporary. The landscape of his childhood was in massive upheaval and change. In parallel, *coming out* was complex in a world that was only just shifting its moral and legal attitudes, making blending-in a survival strategy. Alongside writing and exhibiting, he is Co-founder of g39, an artist-led space in Cardiff, where he works. Recently he was on the judging panel for Artes Mundi 8, a selector for Jerwood Arts Survey II, and served on the Wales in Venice committee. He is currently part of the Representing Wales 2022 Cohort on a mentoring and support programme run by Literature Wales. Twitter: @anthonyshapland

Satterday Shaw's work has been printed in *Meniscus, Mslexia, The London Magazine,* a Chawton House anthology, *Wasafiri, The Yellow Room* and other publications, with stories coming out in a future issue of *Stand* and *Fly on the Wall Press* magazine. Her short fiction has won the Ilkley Festival Short Story Competition and a New Writing North award. Shaw lives in Harlech, lle mae hi'n ddysgu Cymraeg. Twitter: @satterday_shaw

Daniel Patrick Luke Strogen was born in Swansea and grew up in Port Talbot. He has recently earned a Bachelor of Arts degree from Swansea University. Now, post-graduation, he is beginning his training as a schoolteacher. As a student of linguistics, he won the Babel Young Writers' Competition in 2021 for his article on language use in the media. He has been writing since childhood, but '*Cracked*/Duck' is his first short story. Twitter: @DanielStrogen

PARTHIAN

Fiction

Figurehead

CARLY HOLMES
ISBN 978-1-914595-05-9
£10.00 • Paperback

"Carly Holmes is a bewitching writer, and *Figurehead* is a book that's as full of eeriness and enchantment as one could ever wish for." Buzz Magazine

The Incandescent Threads

RICHARD ZIMLER
ISBN 978-1-913640-64-4
£20.00 • Hardback

THE FIFTH NOVEL IN
THE INTERNATIONALLY
BESTSELLING *SEPHARDIC CYCLE*

"Zimler is an honest, powerful writer." The Guardian

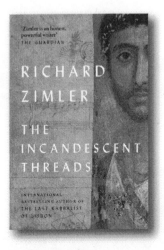

PARTHIAN

Fiction

The Half-life of Snails

PHILIPPA HOLLOWAY
ISBN 978-1-914595-52-3
£9.99 • Paperback

"A careful, tender and arresting story that explores how we're formed by the places we think we own – I was moved by this suspenseful and delicate novel."
Jenn Ashworth

Take a Bite:
The Rhys Davies Short Story Award Anthology

ISBN 978-1-913640-63-7
£9.99 • Paperback

THE TWELVE WINNERS OF THE 2021 RHYS DAVIES SHORT STORY AWARD

PARTHIAN

MODERN WALES

RAYMOND WILLIAMS: A WARRIOR'S TALE

Dai Smith

Raymond Williams (1921-1998) was the most influential socialist writer and thinker in post-war Britain. Now, for the first time, making use of Williams' private and unpublished papers and by placing him in a wide social and cultural landscape, Dai Smith, in this highly original and much praised biography, uncovers how Williams' life to 1961 is an explanation of his immense intellectual achievement.

"Becomes at once the authoritative account... Smith has done all that we can ask the historian as biographer to do."
– Stefan Collini, *London Review of Books*

PB / £16.99
978-1-913640-08-8

FURY OF PAST TIME: A LIFE OF GWYN THOMAS

Daryl Leeworthy

This landmark biography tells the remarkable story of one of modern Wales's greatest literary voices

HB / £20
978-1-914595-19-6

PARTHIAN

RHYS DAVIES

RHYS DAVIES: SELECTED STORIES

Rhys Davies

"Gently wrapped, these stylish perceptive tales have centres as hard as steel, and are all the better for it."
– William Trevor, The Guardian

£8.99 / PB
978-1-912109-78-4

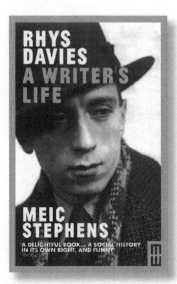

RHYS DAVIES: A WRITER'S LIFE

Meic Stephens

"This is a delightful book, which is itself a social history in its own right, and funny."
– The Spectator

£11.99 / PB
978-1-912109-96-8